KNEADING
the
GRINCH

fabiola francisco

Copyright © 2022 by Fabiola Francisco

All rights reserved.

No portion of this book may be reproduced in any form without written permission from the publisher or author, except as permitted by U.S. copyright law.

BOOKS BY FABIOLA FRANCISCO

Scan the QR Code to find Fabiola's other books!

DEDICATION

For everyone who has felt like they needed a Christmas miracle.

1
AVERY

You know when you see the warning on TV that says, don't try this at home? You should listen. They aren't kidding when they say not to microwave aluminum foil or cut your own hair.

That's how I end up with crooked bangs. Not a slight slant that I can conceal with a side sweep. This is like a three-year-old got a hold of scissors and my hair and went crazy with it.

All I wanted was a change, and how hard could bangs be to cut? Apparently, harder than those online videos make it seem. Grab a chunk of hair, twist, and cut? My ass.

At least you didn't bleach your hair.

But uneven bangs are better than everything else in my life. What should have a huge warning that screams DO NOT TRY THIS AT HOME is marrying a man. Period. That's it.

Right when I thought things were going great, *bam!* Disaster unraveled the string of peace that was holding my life together.

Word of advice: If you're going to get divorced, fight for what belongs to you.

I didn't, and now I live in the small studio apartment above my bakery. Thankfully it has a living space that I've now converted into my home. When my husband—ex-husband—told me he got a job transfer to California, I didn't know how to feel.

I was proud of him, but a pang of sadness hit me at the thought of leaving Emerald Bay.

This beach town may not be the town where I was born, but I've been living here for years, and it's become home.

That didn't matter anyway. The kicker came when he told me he wasn't happy in our marriage and this would be the perfect opportunity to get divorced.

Is there *ever* a perfect opportunity for that? I didn't think so. He, however, was joyous.

How did I miss the signs?

Blowing out a breath, I look at myself in the mirror and cringe. This is not a good look. It's worse than when my mom took me to get a haircut when I was five, and the lady gave me the style of a sixty-year-old woman; short hair all around with the front teased up a bit.

I bet even she could cut straight bangs, though.

My ringing phone is a welcomed distraction. Grabbing it, I grimace when I see my friend's name on the screen.

"Hello?"

"What in the world did you do?" Lizzy's tone is accusing.

Right. I sent her a text message with a picture of scissors and the wispy bangs I wanted.

"Nothing." I sound guilty to my own ears.

"You cut bangs, didn't you?"

"I'm having an existential crisis." I drop onto my couch, lifting my feet on the coffee table.

"I know you're having a hard time, but you're stronger than this. You're definitely stronger than impulse decisions like cutting bangs." She's my voice of reason. If only she'd called prior to hacking away at my hair.

"Everything is a mess. It should be the best time of year for the bakery, and it's not. I'm not sure how I'm going to make it through the end of the year." I voice my biggest fear.

Sprinkles of Joy is all I have left. I can't lose my dream business after all I've already lost. It doesn't help that Matthew is popular in Emerald Bay, and some of the town gossip has painted me as the villain in our divorce.

Gotta love it when rumors start spreading in a small town. And Matthew's not even here to correct it because he's off in California doing god knows what.

"Did I lose you?" Lizzy asks.

"I'm here." I take a deep breath. "I need to go to the bakery and prep for tomorrow. What am I going to do about these bangs?" I stand and walk to the mirror in my bathroom, turning my head this way and that to see how bad the damage is.

It's bad. So, so bad. Like when you get a sunburn, and half your face is peeling while the other is still red like a tomato. I'm adding fuel to the fire now; the gossipers will say I've gone crazy.

"Twist them and clip them back for a couple of weeks until they're long enough, and then you can get a *professional* to fix them."

"Clip them back? What is this, the nineteen-nineties, when everyone used butterfly clips?"

"Nineteen-nineties?" She laughs.

"You know what I mean."

"Use bobby pins, and no one will be able to tell. Gel will help. You've got this, friend." Her encouraging words go beyond a bad haircut.

"I hope so. I really don't want to have to move back to Minnesota with my parents after a failed marriage and career." I set the phone on the bathroom vanity and put it on speaker, turning on the water to rinse my face.

"I won't let that happen. You're a Floridian at heart. Can you imagine how cold it is in Minnesota right now? Probably colder than Antarctica."

I laugh, shaking my head as I dry my face.

"You're ridiculous. It is not that cold, but I do enjoy Florida winters better. Crisp sixty-five-degree weather is my kind of nice. Thanks for checking in. I promise I'll get my life together soon." Lizzy has been a friend through everything.

She and Dani have been my rocks. They were the first friends I made when I moved here after college to live with Matthew, and they haven't wavered no matter what's happened.

"You're welcome. Call me if you need anything. I'm just prepping for class tomorrow. These kids are wild, so I'm trying to keep them in control with fun, educational activities. The pre-Christmas excitement is real."

I laugh at her. Lizzy is a teacher at the elementary school, and from her stories alone, I know I could never do her job.

"Good luck," I say.

"Thanks. Talk to you later."

I hang up and stare at myself again. Determined to not let this get to me, I grab some gel and twist the bangs, slicking them back and holding them in place with a bobby pin. Then, I gel the rest of the top of my head and tie a slick ponytail.

"Not so bad," I tell my reflection.

Feeling a bit lighter, I head down to the bakery to do some work. I'm hoping to turn this bad streak around during the holiday season. I'll need a Christmas miracle, but the last thing I can lose is hope. After all, isn't this the time of year to believe in the unbelievable?

2

AVERY

Christmas music softly plays through the speakers, filling the bakery with a festive feel that I've been missing this year. The colorful lights on the Christmas tree at the entrance of the shop blink, illuminating the ornaments. I have lights strung across the top of the glass display and Christmas decor on the counter, but no matter how much I decorate this place, my mood is still somber. Even my favorite gnomes aren't making me happy.

I rearrange the brownie Christmas trees on the platter for the fifth time this morning. I was so excited about making them, candy cane "tree trunk" included, and yet no one has bought one. Actually, not many people have come in.

The lack of customers shouldn't surprise me anymore, but I once believed that Emerald Bay was the home of community. The town that came together no matter what. I guess once upon a time, I was a local to them. Now, I feel like an outsider.

I'm stuck in my head, organizing the display for the millionth time when the door opens.

"Hi." I smile way too eagerly at the customer.

Tone it down a bit.

I sigh when I see my ex-mother-in-law.

"Hi, dear."

"Hi, Emma. How are you?"

I haven't had much interaction with my ex-in-laws in the past year. They were my family once, but now they're practically strangers.

"I'm good, and you?" She looks around the empty bakery.

"Good, good. Working. You know how it is." I place my palm on the counter to try to seem cool and calm.

Her eyes meet mine with raised eyebrows. She isn't buying it. Anyone can tell that the bakery has lost half its clients. Instead of helping me, she's stayed out of it.

"I came by to talk about something." She frowns as if the news she's going to give me is the most heartbreaking. "Matthew is coming for Christmas."

"I assumed so." I cross my arms, needing a shield.

"He's seeing someone new. She'll be coming with him to meet us."

My blood ices. I'm pretty sure my entire heart freezes over at the news. It's not that I never expected him to move on, especially in a new state. I'm just not ready to see it flaunted in front of me.

"I see. I'm glad he's happy." What else do you tell your ex-mother-in-law? I wish your son still loved me? I'm still recovering from the divorce? The divorce that has caused me to lose more than a relationship.

And the truth is, I don't think I want him to still love me because I've never wanted to be with someone who wasn't one hundred percent sure he loved me.

"He'll be arriving this week, so I wanted you to know. I don't want any..." She eyes me as if I could finish her sentence for her.

"Any what? I'm sorry, Emma, but I'm not a mind reader." My tone is snarky.

"Any problems with them and you."

I tilt my head and sigh. "Emma, you know the divorce was amicable. Did it catch me off-guard? Absolutely. I think even you were surprised at first. However, I've never caused any issues for anyone. I've been friendly, understanding. I let him sell the house so he could move with more money in his pocket. What else do people want from me?" I throw my hands up, exasperated.

"Calm down."

"I am calm. What I hate is everyone thinking I'm some crazy, obsessed ex-wife. You could've helped with that, you know? Helped by extinguishing the rumors before they got out of hand."

"You know we didn't want to get involved."

I snort at her tired excuse.

"Don't worry. I won't even talk to Matthew. There's really no reason to besides a cordial hello if we cross each other on the street. I'll be on my best behavior." I smile. Yeah, there's a hint of sarcasm in there, but who cares. I'm the one in a bind.

"Thank you," she says. Then she looks at the display, opens her mouth, and closes it again.

"Do you want something?" I push because I am that desperate to make a sale this morning.

"No, thank you." She walks away, leaving me once again alone with a full display of sweet treats, including holiday specialties that may go to waste.

I just hope children show up for the gingerbread house decorating class on Saturday. The last thing I want is for Matthew to hear how bad business is. I'm too proud for him to think I'm failing at a dream he questioned.

The timing was perfect since the previous bakery owner was retiring and hadn't found a replacement. I thought it was a sign from above. And it was amazing up until about seven months ago.

I look up when the door opens again and hold my breath. The last thing I need is for Matthew's dad to come in and warn me as well. I think at that point I might go crazy-ex like people think.

"Hey, there, buddy." Dani walks in with a bright smile, although I see a hint of laughter in her eyes.

"Hey."

"How are you doing?" She tilts her head. "Anything exciting happening?"

My shoulders drop, and I scowl. "You spoke to Lizzy, didn't you?"

"Yeah." She throws her head back and laughs. "Let me see the damage."

"No. I got it under control with gel and bobby pins. I am not showing you the sorry excuse for bangs."

"You're no fun." She pouts, but that won't work on me. "Anyway…" She walks up to the display, eyeing everything like a hungry tiger.

"Can I get a dozen donuts and one of those Christmas trees?"

"You got it. Do you want glazed, or do you want to try my gingerbread donuts? They're filled with a gingerbread cream and topped with cinnamon sugar." I'm selling these hard because they are delicious.

She licks her lips, and I laugh.

"That sounds so good. I'll do half and half. And I'll have the brownie now. If people at the station see me with it, they'll try to steal it." She reaches her hand out for the brownie like a greedy child. "Thanks," she adds and takes a bite, closing her eyes dramatically. "So good," she says around a mouth full of chocolate.

I package a dozen donuts and ring her up. I'm grateful my friends are still supporting me, even when they don't have to. I know Dani doesn't need to come in and buy donuts for the radio station her dad owns, but she won't let me lose this fight.

"Thanks for stopping by, even if you were hoping to make fun of me."

"That's what friends are for. Who else would mock you if not a friend?" She giggles at her own joke and grabs the box. "We'll talk later. If I'm late, my dad will kill me." She rushes off, leaving me with a smile.

The rest of the morning passes with a bit of activity. I'm glad there are people in town that I can still count on. It helps to ease the burden when it becomes too heavy to carry.

"Hello." An unfamiliar, deep voice hits my back as I push forward the packs of Christmas cookies that are on the shelves behind the display.

"Hello?" I turn around and see a man dressed in gray fitted slacks and a white Oxford shirt with the sleeves rolled up a couple of times, exposing what looks very much like a Rolex.

His green eyes sweep down my body as far as he can see with the display in front of me.

"How can I help you?"

"Right." He clears his throat and steps forward. "I'm Gabriel Hill, owner of Sweet Delights." He reaches his hand out, but I just cross my arms and stare at him.

"Sweet Delights? The bakery chain?"

"One and the same." His wolf-like smile irks me. It screams salesperson.

I lift my brows and continue to stare, unsure about what he's doing here unless he wants to buy something.

"Anyway, I'm looking to expand my stores to the area, and I would like to schedule a meeting with you to—"

"I'm unavailable," I interrupt him and stand tall, but my heart is racing.

"I'd just like to talk."

"Not happening." I shake my head for emphasis. "If you want to bring a franchise into this town, you're going to have a hard time. People here like to support their locals."

"First of all, it's not a franchise. It's a chain of bakeries. Secondly, from my research, business hasn't been going well. I can help."

My nostrils flare, and I walk around the counter, pressing my finger into his chest.

"I don't care what research you've done. As a businessman, you should know every business goes through some challenges, but that doesn't mean I need saving."

Gabriel lifts his hands and steps back. "I'll come back another day."

"Don't bother," I spit out.

The last thing I need is for some successful stranger to come in and buy the bakery from me. I may not have fought for my marriage, but I'm not giving up on my dreams.

"Okay." He steps farther back. "I'll come back another day."

"With all due respect, you're wasting your time."

"We'll see about that." He smirks and walks away.

I slump against the display and release a deep exhale. As if I didn't have enough, now this guy comes around flashing his expensive watch, leaving a trail of his foresty cologne, and telling me he can help my business. More like *steal* it.

I stare at the angel on top of my Christmas tree and frown.

"Any chance you can help with a miracle?" I talk to the inanimate object.

The crazy thing is that I keep looking at it as if it'll respond. I've lost my marbles.

A *Sweet Delights location.* I shake my head. As if I'd sell this place so they can put in a mass market bakery that may not even sell fresh goods.

Gabriel Hill can run off toward the hills.

3

GABRIEL

I INHALE THE SALTY air as I walk along the beach. Emerald Bay is a unique place with its charming small-town atmosphere bordered by the ocean. I haven't visited in years, and although some things have changed, its essence remains the same.

When my grandparents lived here, I'd come stay with them for a few weeks during the summer. Coming from Denver, Emerald Bay was an escape that provided the freedom I didn't really get back home.

I take a seat on a bench near the beach and check my phone. I go over the notes I have about Sprinkles of Joy. It's been open since the previous bakery closed five years ago when Avery bought it.

She was tough as nails. Tougher than I gave her credit for when my sources told me the bakery in town was drowning.

I'm not sure why if Emerald Bay has always loved their baked goods. All I can assume is that Avery isn't offering the people what they want. I may not be a native of this town either, but I know the people.

I don't have much more information aside from knowing she's freshly divorced. A life-altering change like that could affect someone's business, so that may be the blame for the decrease in sales.

Regardless of why her business is failing, I can offer to buy her place for its location alone. The storefront is prime real estate that's near the boardwalk; it's a common area tourists frequent during the winter and summer.

Emerald Bay is an oasis at all times of the year, with comfortable winter temperatures and warm summer months.

My phone buzzes in my hand, stopping my admiration of the ocean. I answer when I see Luke's name on the screen. He's the closest person I have here. My grandparents were his neighbor, so I spent many summers playing with him as a kid.

"Hey." I lean back on the bench, crossing my ankle over my knee.

"Hey, man, what's up?"

"Not much, sitting by the beach. Are you off work?" Luke is a deputy sheriff in town, and his schedule is all sorts of chaotic some days.

"Just got out. Want to grab a bite to eat and catch up? You've been in town for a few days, and we still haven't had a chance to hang out."

"Yeah, that'd be great. Want to meet in an hour?" I stand, heading toward my car.

"Works for me. Is Jim's okay?" He sounds farther away now, and I assume he's put the phone on speaker.

"Yeah. I'll see you then." I hang up and get in my car, excited about catching up with Luke.

I'm hoping to spend a couple weeks here before heading back home for Christmas Eve. That should be enough time to meet with Avery and make a deal we can close after New Year's.

I stop at my grandparents' old house, which I inherited, and grab my laptop to send Avery an e-mail with my proposal. If she won't talk to me now, maybe she will after she sees what I'm willing to pay.

Money always talks.

I'm determined to close this deal, so as stubborn as she thinks she is, she's no match for me. Re-reading the e-mail, I send it and close my laptop, ready to spend time with an old friend.

Not long after, Luke and I are sitting at a table in Jim's and catching up on the recent years. It seems like life has been good to him, and he's happy with his job. I never thought Luke would end up in the law enforcement field back when we were growing up. He spent a fair share of time trespassing through properties to get to the beach faster instead of weaving through neighborhoods.

Some of my best memories were made in this town. My family is amazing, and I love them, but this place is magical.

"No such luck with Avery, then?" Luke wipes his hands and grabs his glass to take a drink of Coke.

"Nope, but I'm not giving up."

"I'm not sure she's willing to sell, but it's worth a try. It could help her if business is as bad as people say." He shrugs, grabbing a fry from his plate.

I take a bite of my burger, tossing his words around. She didn't seem willing to sell, but what's the point of keeping a place that is drowning you?

"I'm going to see her again tomorrow. I e-mailed her my proposal and am hopeful she'll accept. If business is bad, then it'd be a mistake to pass up this offer."

"Aren't you afraid that business will be bad for you, too?" He tilts his head.

"You told me she's had problems since she got divorced. I'm guessing it's something personal." Luke didn't hesitate to mention Avery's divorce seems to be why her business hasn't been going well.

"We have friends in common, and she's a great person. I'm not sure why people in town are gossiping." He shakes his head.

"Small town charm." I smile.

"Whatever. Are you headed back to Colorado for Christmas, or are your parents coming down?"

"I'm headed that way. My brother's going to be in town, too, so we're doing a whole family reunion." I chuckle.

I haven't seen Ben in months since we live in different states. The last time I saw him, I was in Arizona checking out one of my storefronts, and we were able to meet for lunch.

"Sounds like fun."

"It should be. You're staying in town, I assume?" I look at him as I finish off my burger

"Yup. My parents are here, and I'll have to work during the holidays. No calling in sick for me. The gossipers in town will rat me out." He laughs.

"I can imagine. No one could get away with a secret affair in this place."

"Hell no. Someone tried to get away with that, and I don't think it was a secret after a week. And it only lasted that long because they started their affairs by meeting out of town."

"Damn."

"I know. Nothing gets past Emerald Bay residents. I don't even try." He smiles.

I laugh, understanding what he means. I remember my grandma always complaining about people gossiping without a foundation of the truth.

We finish up and pay for dinner before heading out.

"I'm glad we got together." I clap Luke's shoulder. "Let's try to see each other before I leave again. Although, once I have my store here, I'll be in town more often."

Luke laughs, slapping my back.

"Mighty confident there. I'd try to get Avery to talk to you before you get ahead of yourself. But deal, we'll hang out again before you leave."

I shake his hand and leave, hoping I have some news from Avery. I check my e-mail once I'm home and hurriedly open the message from her. I snort when I read her words.

Gabriel,

I'm not for sale. I mean...my business is not for sale. Although, I'm not for sale either. Sprinkles of Joy is my dream, and I'm sure you can understand that dreams are priceless. Go back where you came from. You're wasting your time.

Avery

We'll see about that, Avery. I like a challenge, and you just placed one on a silver platter for me.

4
AVERY

I FINISH RINGING UP a customer with a smile, glad I've had a bit more business today. I'm looking at the bright side while still begging the Christmas tree angel for a miracle that does not involve Gabriel from Sweet Delights.

The door chimes with a new customer, and I glance up happily—until I see who it is; instantly, my smile drops. My eyes meet those of a man who knows everything about me but has become a complete stranger. And his new girlfriend is standing beside him.

"Oh, my! This place is adorable, babe," his girlfriend shrieks.

I wait for her to say something sarcastic, but her compliment sounds genuine.

"Hi." His voice still has the same deep timbre I remember.

"Hey." I press my lips together.

The few customers in the bakery look between us with wide eyes as if they have just won the lottery. I mean, they did win the Emerald Bay gossip lottery. A lot of people would pay big bucks to have front-row seats to my reunion with Matthew.

"Jessy wanted to come in and buy something." He points to his girlfriend, who has her arm looped around his, as if I knew who she was.

"Right. Well, welcome, welcome." I clap my hands and cringe.

"Hi, it's so nice to meet you." Jessy releases his arm and speed-walks to me, hand extended.

I lift my brows and lean back, unsure of what the hell is going on. Did I wake up in an alternate universe? That could be it. This world isn't my real life.

"This may be awkward, but I've heard so much about you and wanted to meet you. Besides, I am *obsessed* with sweets, so this is a double treat. Ha! *Treat*. You get it?" She snorts, and I shake my thoughts away.

"It's nice to meet you, too." I shake her hand.

She's pretty, with faint freckles sprinkled on the bridge of her nose and cheeks, auburn hair, and expressive brown eyes. The worst part is that she seems nice. Like really nice.

Ugh. This would be my luck.

Matthew stays behind, hands in his pockets, looking at the interaction. My heart is racing, and I'm wondering how to even react in this moment. The last thing I want is for him to witness that people aren't shopping here.

"All of this looks delicious. Doesn't it, Matty?" She looks at him over her shoulder, and I lift my eyebrows, holding back my laughter.

He definitely never liked the nickname Matty. I guess people change in relationships. Regardless, it's not my problem. It's clear he's moved on, and I...I kind of have. The fact that I have a failed marriage under my belt stings. No one in my family has ever been divorced before, and I never thought I'd be the first.

"It does." He nods, eyeing me impassively. "How have you been?" His hand goes to the small of Jessy's back.

I can't help but zero in on the action. Not long ago, it was my back he was touching.

Really, Avery? A back?

"Good, great. Things have been fantastic here." I spread my arms wide. "Work is great." I exaggerate the word great and internally grimace. I hope it didn't sound forced to him.

"Really? I thought—"

"Oh! Would you look who's here?" I rush to the door, not one bit sorry for cutting Matthew off. I'm carelessly acting on impulse.

My heart is beating so fast; I feel like I've sprinted a million yards. Forget the Olympics. I'm ready for the Guinness World Record.

Gabriel's eyes widen, probably at my insane smile. He's going to regret stepping into this bakery right now. Maybe this will scare him away afterward.

"Honey, you're here. Come on and meet some friends." I wrap my arm around his waist and look at him.

His eyebrows quirk in question, and I keep my smile in place while I whisper, "Play along."

"Matthew, Jessy, this is Gabriel." I introduce them while a warning bell rings in the back of my mind, telling me to abandon ship.

"Uh..." Matthew's eyebrows lift. "I didn't know you were seeing someone."

"You don't know everything about me, silly." I slap his shoulder. "I didn't know about Jessy until your mom came in yesterday and warned me." If someone took a picture of my face right now, I'm sure I'd look crazier than a drunk clown.

"It's, uh, nice to meet you." Gabriel shakes Matthew's hand.

He looks terrified, and I can't blame him. I just dragged him into this uncomfortable situation. I don't even know the guy.

"Yeah, likewise."

"This is so great." Jessy claps her hands. "The four of us should have dinner together. Matthew's told me the pizza in town is amazing, and I'm dying to try it. What do you say, Matty?"

Gabriel laughs, and I elbow his ribs, causing him to cough.

"Oh, sorry, sweetie. Are you okay?" I rub his arm, feigning that I care.

"I'm fine," he bites.

"Anyway, I'm actually really busy and wake up really early to bake before opening the bakery, but you should definitely try House of Pies. It's delicious."

"Oh, come on." Jessy pouts, and I have a feeling she isn't used to not getting what she wants. "We can meet right after you close and be done early. I've been wanting to meet you. You could tell me all the secrets Matty will keep from me since you know him better."

This time Matthew coughs, covering his mouth in an attempt to hide his red face.

"Jessy," he warns. "They're busy. What do you want to order?"

"You're no fun." She turns her pout to him. "How's six for dinner? You close at five-thirty, so it should be plenty of time."

I look at Gabriel and his wide eyes.

"We, uh, actually can't." I shake my head as if I'm so sorry that I'll miss this dinner. I'd rather eat week-old soggy cookies than go through this dinner.

"You know what, sweetie? I think I can cancel our previous arrangement. It's not every day we get to enjoy a meal with old friends." Gabriel's face has transformed from surprised shock to dangerous.

"I don't think we can cancel our previous engagement," I say through clenched teeth.

"Of course. I'll just send a message and reschedule." The weasel grabs his phone and pretends to type something before smiling at us. "Done. We'll see you at six."

Matthew opens and closes his mouth while I wish the earth would open up and swallow me.

"Sounds great," Jessy shrieks.

"Excuse me?" A customer says at the counter, and I realize I'm at work with an audience.

Fuck my life sideways.

"Oh, sorry." I head to the back of the counter and serve her while keeping my eyes on Gabriel, Matthew, and Jessy. She's talking a mile a minute, waving her hands around, and laughing.

"I heard he was home for the holidays with a new girlfriend." The customer leans in and whispers.

"Yeah." I swallow past the lump in my throat that carries the memories I've tried to store in the back of my mind, hidden deep in my subconscious.

"Thanks, dear."

"You're welcome. Merry Christmas." I smile at her.

"I hope you don't mind that I sprung dinner on you like that." Jessy grips the counter and leans forward a bit.

"Not at all," I say.

"Anyway, can I have a Christmas tree brownie? They're adorable. I think brownies with frosting are an underrated combination." I grab the brownie with the green frosting and package it for her.

"Here you go. Hope you like it."

"I'm sure I will. See you tonight." She heads back to Matthew, and they leave.

I blow out a deep breath and sag against the counter. No amount of deep meditation breaths are going to slow down my heartbeat.

"Well, that was fun."

I glower at the man I'd like to kill.

"Why did you agree to that?"

"Why did you pretend I was your boyfriend?"

"Have you never panicked before? I saw you and acted on impulse. I don't know." I throw my hands in the air before covering my face. I want to cry and laugh at the same time.

Instead of a Christmas miracle, I'm entering a Christmas nightmare.

"It's clear you were in an uncomfortable situation. I'm not sure what is going on, but I'd guess that Matthew is your ex-husband."

I peek at him through my fingers and sigh. "Even you know I'm divorced?"

"Word travels fast, and I'm not a total stranger to Emerald Bay. I can help you out." His smile is dazzling, and hope fills me. I don't want to admit I made up a fake boyfriend because I felt inferior. "I'll play along while he's here if you give me a chance."

Face drops. "I'm not looking to date."

"A chance at my proposal." He shakes his head.

"You know what? My pride isn't that important to me. I'll just tell them we broke up. Unexpectedly. We've been fighting a lot, and things have been tense, and you got super jealous of my ex-husband. It'll be fine. Everything will be fine." I start to panic, my breath coming in short spurts. I press the heel of my palm into my chest and bend over, trying to catch my breath.

"Breathe, Avery." He rubs my arms.

"I can't," I say on a gasp.

"Look, you don't have to accept my deal yet. While we pretend to be dating in front of your ex, you give me a chance to tell you all about Sweet Delights and my plans. Who knows, you might love the idea so much you'd beg me for a job."

I stare at him blankly and unimpressed, but Gabriel simply smiles.

"I'm going to regret this. And it doesn't mean I'm agreeing to sell." I point a finger at him.

"We can work together for a week and see how things go. I'll show you how I'd run this place if it were mine."

"No. I'm still the owner and have a reputation to uphold."

"Fifty, fifty." He extends his hand. "It's this or have the entire town spreading a rumor that you were so desperate to one-up your ex-husband that you made up a fake boyfriend."

"Ugh." I roll my eyes. "Deal." We shake hands, and I ignore the way his fits in mine. It's a silly thing to observe because we aren't puzzle pieces.

"You won't regret this."

"Doubtful." I take a deep breath and shake off this feeling that things are about to blow up in my face.

5

GABRIEL

Jessy talks a lot. With her hands. And in a high-pitched, excited voice. I don't miss the way people stare at our table as if we're science experiments about to collide into mass destruction.

Matthew is quiet while his girlfriend talks, though I don't miss the way he looks at Avery with an odd expression as if he's trying to get a read on her but it's in a foreign language.

I wonder if he's onto us, but I had to take advantage of the situation to spin this into something that would benefit me. Some people may call me a user, but the opportunity presented itself; I would've been a fool to let it pass me by.

It's fate. That's how I'm looking at it. After all, we're in the holiday season, and it's the time of year things work under a magical spell or something. At least that's what the movies my mom loves to watch on Hallmark depict.

Speaking of Hallmark...the restaurant sure is decorated like something straight out of one of their festive movies. Ornaments galore with Santa figures, gnomes, and stars, blinking lights, and Christmas music plays from the speakers. The waiters are even wearing Christmas hats.

"Honey, don't you love lemon cake, too?" I ask Avery when Jessy talks all about the Starbucks lemon cake she's obsessed with and how she tried to recreate it but failed.

"Do you know how to make it?" Jessy's eyes widen. "If so, I'd love to order one. Wouldn't that be great for Christmas brunch?" She looks at Matthew with a loving smile.

"Lemon during Christmas?" He tilts his head. "I guess, but Avery doesn't like lemon in desserts." He smirks in a condescending way. Like he knows Avery better than I do.

While that is true, I can play along.

"Actually, tastes change, and Gabe has shown me that lemon dessert is actually amazing." Avery smiles at me, placing her hand over mine. "Isn't that right?" I shouldn't let her deep gaze pull me in, or her hand over mine make me feel anything other than neutral.

"You bake?" Matthew's brows furrow.

"I do. I went to culinary school." This time I can tell the truth, and I don't miss the slight quirk in Avery's eyebrows before she collects herself.

"It's something that really helped us to bond."

"I thought you had just arrived in town." Matthew leans back in his chair.

"I grew up visiting in the summers, so I'm not unfamiliar with Emerald Bay. Maybe you remember my grandparents? Louise and Harold? They lived on Palm Street next to Luke Barber."

"Louise and Harold. Yeah, I remember them. Wow, so you're their grandchild. From Idaho or something, right?"

"Colorado," I correct him.

"Yeah, yeah, the Midwest." He waves me off.

I hold back from rolling my eyes, wondering if this guy is just an ass to me or if it's just his natural persona.

"Excuse me?" Avery crosses her arms. "You never had anything negative to say about the Midwest. Or have you forgotten where I come from?" Her voice is stern as she glares at him.

"Of course not." Matthew shakes his head as if he's been chastised.

So Avery is from the Midwest.

"And while I have nothing against the Midwest, *Colorado* is actually in the Rocky Mountains region, not the Midwest. Maybe you confused it for *Chicago*. That's in Illinois." I smile, mocking him, and grab another slice of pizza. Avery was right. This pizza is amazing.

"Right, well, it's right at the cut-off. Geography isn't my strong suit." He shrugs unapologetically.

"I do love Colorado. We could go skiing there this winter." Jessy looks at Matthew, and I finally see him smile genuinely.

Maybe this situation is making him as uncomfortable as the rest of us, provoking his asshole ways. But the guy has moved on, so he has no right to be jealous of his ex being with someone new. He brought his new girlfriend to meet the parents. That's a big deal, in my opinion. The only girlfriend who met my parents was an old college one.

"That would be great," he tells Jessy and goes back to his pizza.

"Skiing is great. Isn't it so fun? I love it," Avery rambles on beside me, looking like a deer in headlights. "When I was a kid, I wanted to snowboard, so my parents took me to lessons, and I could barely stand on the board. One movement and I'd fall. But skiing, yeah, that's great. You know, both feet aren't stuck to the same board, so it's easier to move around."

I sneak my hand under the table and squeeze her knee to shut her up. If she keeps on going, she's going to prove that this is affecting her, and for some reason, I feel bad for her.

If the rumors are true that business is bad due to her divorce, she doesn't need people adding to that by witnessing a hot mess double date.

Her eyes snap to mine, and she grabs my hand and removes it from her knee. I chuckle at her reaction. At least it got her to be quiet.

"Avery, tell me everything about the bakery. What's your favorite recipe to make?" Jessy leans forward.

"Um, it depends on my mood. I'm definitely a mood baker, but I have a specialty, which is a recipe my grandmother taught me. Every time I make it, I think of her."

"What is it?" Jessy clasps her and waits impatiently.

Avery glances at me and then back at Jessy. "If I tell you, I'd have to kill you." She laughs at her joke, but Jessy scoots back and looks at her with her nose scrunched.

"It's a quote from *Top Gun*." Avery looks at her as if it were obvious. "It's a joke," she adds.

"I've never seen *Top Gun*. Sorry." Jessy shrugs.

Avery shakes her head as if this couldn't be real and says, "It's a butter pecan cookie recipe with a twist, but the twist is a family secret."

"Oh, wow, that's interesting."

Avery looks at me again with narrowed eyes. Is she afraid I'm going to steal her recipe? I may have taken advantage of the situation, but I'd never take a recipe that isn't mine.

"Well, this has been fun, but I'm sure you're tired. Should we grab the bill?" Matthew claps his hands and wraps his arm around Jessy.

"Yeah, good idea." Avery leans into me in an attempt to cuddle but miscalculates.

Like in slow motion, she topples to the side, screaming and landing between both of our chairs in a weird twist.

"Are you okay?" I scoot back and bend to help her while people laugh quietly.

"Yeah, but you could've caught me or something," she hisses.

"Sorry, I didn't realize what was happening until it did." I shake my head, whispering our conversation.

I grab her hand and help her up while Jessy comes to our side to help as well.

"Avery, oh no! Are you okay? I can take a look if you're hurt. I'm a nurse."

"Of course you are," Avery mutters, and I hold back a chuckle. "I'm okay."

Her face is red as she brushes her hands off on her jeans and keeps her eyes cast downward.

"Anyway, it is getting late. We should pay and go." She sits back down, keeping her head bowed.

People at tables nearby whisper and look at her. Sympathy hits me, and I can't help but feel bad for her. Just from observation, anyone can tell that this situation is eating at her. I wave down the waiter and pay our bill quickly to get her out of here. She's had enough embarrassment.

"I could've paid my part." Avery crosses her arms and looks at me once we're outside.

"I'm sure, but then it would ruin our façade. Or people will talk and say that your date is cheap, and I am anything but that." I shift on my feet and smile at her. "Are you sure you're okay?"

"A bruised ego is nothing new to me. I'm sure mine is permanently black and blue at this point." She waves me off, acting stronger than her eyes reflect. She can try to fool me, but I can see the way her eyes crinkle with sadness, and her breath is slow and deep.

She shivers and tightens her jacket around her body.

"If my family saw me shaking in sixty-degree weather, they'd laugh at me. Anyway, thanks for dinner. I guess I'll have to see you around." Her lips purse.

"You'll see me tomorrow. You have your side of the deal to uphold." I wink.

"You mean you didn't forget about that?" Her smile is false and wide.

"Not a chance, Rudolph."

"Excuse me?" Her eyebrows lift as she glares at me.

"Your nose is red. You reminded me of Rudolph." I shrug.

"Do you want me to show you my hooves then?" Her hands go to her waist, and I eye the way her hip pops to the side, accentuating her curves. This situation we're in isn't easy, but I can't deny that she's sexy as hell.

"No, I'm sure I can live without seeing them."

"Okay, Grinch." She rolls her eyes.

"Please enlighten me with the nickname because I actually like Christmas."

"Because you're here to ruin *my* Christmas." She takes a deep breath, dropping her arms and tucking them into the pockets of her jeans.

"I promise my intention is to sweeten your Christmas." I shift on my feet, smirking.

"I think we have different definitions for sweet."

"I'll prove you wrong." I rub my hands together. "Now, let's get you home."

"You don't have to walk me. I know the way." She turns and walks away.

I stare at her for a moment, smiling like a fool. She's a fun challenge. Racing to catch up, I walk her home despite her arguments. I'm a gentleman, after all. Even if she thinks I'm her Grinch.

6
AVERY

I ROLL OUT THE cookie dough and use my Christmas tree cookie cutter to cut out the shapes. I'm up to my elbows in flour and sugar, literally, and I'm pretty sure my face is dirty, too. It's my usual look on workdays.

When the oven beeps, I race to take out the red velvet cake I'm baking as today's cake of the day. When the cake pan is on the cooling rack, I get back to my task. "Home for the Holidays" plays from my music app, and I hum along, swaying to the beat as I organize the cookies on a sheet pan. Once those are in the oven, I work on cupcakes.

I'm feeling inspired. Or better yet, taking out my emotions on baking. Dinner last night was so weird. It felt like I was in the *Twilight Zone*.

First, it was strange to have dinner with Matthew as anything but the husband and wife we once were. Sitting across from him while Jessy spoke, watching him smile at her and hold her hand. It was crushing. I tried to keep up a strong front, but I don't know if I was convincing.

I know Matthew and I are over, but how do you overcome a twelve-year relationship in seven months? It's not that easy when you see the person with someone else but want to act out of instinct. Like when he had tomato sauce on his chin, I'd always be the one to tell him. Now, he has someone else who is in charge of taking care of him.

I shake my head and hands, dough flying around me, but I'll clean it up later. Right now, I need to focus on my work. I hope that people seeing us at dinner will realize there's no feud between us and start coming back to the bakery.

When "All I Want for Christmas" comes on, I sing along with Mariah Carey, dancing around and cleaning up once everything is finished. Using the broom as a microphone, I sweep the kitchen and head to the front of the store to make sure everything is neatly displayed.

My eyes scan the seating area to make sure the tables are set. I jump back and scream when I see a figure at the glass door. My hand grips my apron at my chest as my heart jackhammers. Turning on the lights, I see Gabriel's face through the hole in the wreath hanging on the door and mumble a curse while opening the door.

Not creepy at all. Is this the Christmas season or Halloween?

"Your mission is to give me a heart attack one day at a time, right? First, buying me out. Now, standing like some creep at the door?" I arch an eyebrow.

"I was distracted by your dancing skills. Please, don't stop on my account. Your lips were moving, so go ahead and continue singing as well." He smirks, walking into the bakery.

"I'm not open yet."

"I'm not a customer. We have a deal, remember?" He walks around the counter, making himself at home. I don't like the way he moves around here with so much ease. It's as if he already owns the place.

"I need to work."

"I'll help. Where do you keep the aprons? I want one like yours with a Christmas tree on it." He points to me.

"I don't have another one, but..." An idea forms, and I move to the kitchen, grabbing my green apron and writing down the word Grinch on a name tag. "Here you go!"

"Really?" He tilts his head.

"All for the holiday spirit."

"Okay. If you think this is going to scare me off, you're wrong." He ties the apron around his back, his arms flexing beneath the sleeves of his Henley. A shirt shouldn't be sexy, but seeing it on Gabriel makes me think fabric can make someone desirable.

"Did you really go to culinary school?" I blurt out to distract myself from his strong arms.

"Yeah. How do you think I got into the pastry business?" His eyes lift to mine.

"I don't know. I thought you were just a businessman using culinary chefs to expand your success." I slide the glass display door closed and turn to look at him.

"I work in what I know. I started the first Sweet Delights on my own, learning everything about the business. Then I expanded in the city until I could grow throughout the country.

"And now you want to flaunt your success to me." I sigh, unimpressed.

"I'm not here to flaunt it. I want to open a location in Emerald Bay. I could've just bought a different place and stolen your customers, but I'm offering you a better opportunity."

"Am I supposed to be grateful?"

Gabriel sighs, running a hand through his hair. His minty breath hits my face while I wait for a response.

"Let me show you what I have to offer. That was our agreement."

"Fine," I breathe out.

I can't risk him turning his back on me and telling people our date was just a frantic ruse. I'm certain I don't want to sell, so I just need to tolerate Gabriel for two weeks. I can do this. And maybe if people see me spending time with him, they'll realize there's no foundation to the horrid divorce, and my business will boom again.

"I always have samples at my bakeries. It draws people in for the free bite, and then they buy what they love. Have you thought about offering that? It could help pull the customers you lost back in." He's grabbing the cupcake platter closer to him on the counter, and I watch him warily.

"I've never had to offer free stuff for people to come in." My shoulders sag. Having the only bakery in town, coupled with being Matthew's wife, had advantages I wouldn't have anywhere else.

"Times change. Are you going to roll with the changes or let them swallow you up?" His eyes stare into mine for too long.

"Why are you giving me advice on how to succeed? Don't you want me to fail so I'll desperately sell to you?" This doesn't make sense.

"If I just let you fail, then I won't prove my worth. If this is your baby, then you'll want it in good hands." His eyebrow quirks when he finishes off his sentence, and I look away from his intense gaze.

"I know how to run my business."

"I never said you didn't, but something's not working. With the money I pay you, you can open a new Sprinkles of Joy somewhere else." He leans against the back counter, crossing his ankle over his foot.

"I don't want a bakery somewhere else."

"So you want to keep living here even after getting divorced when you don't have any family here?" He lifts his hands as if the idea were absurd.

"I have friends here. I like living in Emerald Bay."

"Right." He nods and pushes off the counter.

A knock at the door startles us both, and I look over to see Mrs. Daniels waiting impatiently outside with her purse hanging from her arm as she rubs her hands together.

"Come on, Rudolph, be my guiding light." Gabriel rubs my head, and I slap his hand away. The last thing I need is for my bangs disaster to come to light and for everyone to see it.

I unlock the door, letting Mrs. Daniels in.

"Good morning, Mrs. Daniels." I attempt a smile, wondering why she's here.

She was one of my regulars and then stopped coming altogether. Betrayal hurts, and I can't quite make my smile feel real.

"Hello, dear. I've missed your sweets. I was on a diet, so I had to cut back, but calories don't count during the holiday season." She winks, walking up to the display to eye what I have, but her gaze lingers on Gabriel.

She wasn't on a diet. I saw her at Bay Brew with a large coffee, devouring a muffin more times than I can count. Some people have no shame.

"I see you've got a new helper." Her eyes cut to mine for a moment before taking Gabriel in with a slow sweep.

"Something like that," I mumble and move to serve her. "What would you like?"

"So many goodies. It all looks delicious. Oh! Are those your butter pecan cookies? I'll take four of those." Her nail taps on the glass. "This cake looks so moist." I cringe at her use of the word like an immature girl, but I read too much romance to take that word seriously. It's a big no-no in my vocabulary.

After ordering a slice of the red velvet cake and half a dozen donuts as well as the cookies, she grabs her wallet.

"You caught yourself a handsome man." Her chin lifts toward Gabriel, who has been a silent observer.

"What? Oh, no." I shake my head.

"I thought you were on a date yesterday with Matthew and his new girlfriend?" Mrs. Daniels lifts her brows, ready for me to spill the tea.

"Oh, yeah, yeah. Of course, but we're starting to date. We'll see if he makes it official during the holidays." I smile over at Gabriel. "Right, darling?"

"Absolutely." He blows me a kiss. I scowl at him before turning my head to smile at her.

"I'm so happy to hear that. I never did believe those rumors." She leans in and whispers.

"Of course not, Mrs. Daniels." I hold back my eye-roll because she definitely believed them. Her lack of support proves it.

"Hope to see you again soon." She waves her fingers. "Nice to meet you..." She stares at Gabriel expectantly.

"Gabe."

"Gabe. I like it." She nods, walking out of the bakery.

I blow out a breath, and Gabriel tosses his head back, laughing loudly. I glare at him, unamused. I don't have a chance to tell him anything, though, because another customer walks in.

7

GABRIEL

"You owe me a thank you." I look at Avery as she eats her sandwich.

"Excuse me?" She says around a mouthful. "Sorry," she mumbles, covering her mouth.

"I'm not allergic to rude eating behaviors," I joke, which earns me about the fiftieth eye-roll of the day so far.

"Why would I thank you?" She wipes her mouth.

"Because people are coming in to find out who I am, and they're buying because they know they can't just show up and interview us." I cross my arms.

"All I wanted was to seem like I had moved on. Somehow, the entire town is now curious about our non-relationship." She takes the last bite of her sandwich.

"I beg to differ. We have a business relationship."

That earns me another eye-roll.

"Ah, eye-roll number fifty-one." Ruffling her feathers is way too much fun.

"Gabriel, while I appreciate your help, I am not a fan of your mocking."

"Okay, I'll cool it." I lift my hands in mock surrender. "Tomorrow, we run things my way, making my recipes. You won't steal them, right?" I jab her.

"Of course not. But I have a gingerbread house decorating class for kids on Saturday. It's non-negotiable."

"I like the idea. Have you thought about teaming up with the coffee shop and buying a traveler box of coffee to give away a cup with the purchase of a donut? Or the florist? You can sell a bouquet of flowers and a cake or cupcake as a gift for a loved one on special occasions like birthdays, anniversaries, or graduations." I toss out different ideas, many things we do at Sweet Delights.

Avery stares at me unmoving, but I can see her tossing around these ideas with the way she chews her bottom lip and slightly narrows her eyes as if she were concentrating on something.

"I don't want to steal any customers from Bay Brew."

"You won't. You'll be buying the coffee from them, and realistically, it would be enough for the first twelve to fifteen customers. It will reel them in with a sense of urgency and bragging rights that they got the free coffee."

She snorts, shaking her head. "Lately, I'm lucky if I get twelve customers in one day." Her jaw clenches.

"You've gotten more today. You called me Grinch, but I should be nicknamed your Lucky Charm."

"Ha, ha, ha." Her sarcasm makes me smile.

"I'm just speaking the truth." I hold my arms out.

Avery throws away the aluminum foil her sandwich was wrapped in, and I use the moment to take her in without her glowering at me. She's beautiful, but the stress of her business weighs on her. Her shoulders are tight, and she stretches her back often as if trying to unload the pressure she's under.

"The flower shop idea is a good one." She finally speaks. Instead of looking at me, she's wiping down the counter.

"It'd help both businesses, so I don't see why they wouldn't agree. I can go—"

"No. I'll go." She lifts her hand.

"Okay, so I'll stay and man the bakery." I have a feeling she won't like that option either.

"Maybe I can call Brianna after work. Yeah, that's what I'll do."

I shake my head. "I'm not gonna do anything behind your back. I've been very forthcoming. It's not like I'm hiding the fact that I want to buy this place."

"I still don't trust you." She stares at me.

"It's a shame. I'm very trustworthy. I thought I'd proven that at dinner last night."

"Don't let that go to your head. It was a moment of weakness." She turns up the volume on the song and hums.

"Where did you go to school?" I ask her over the music.

"Tennessee."

"And that's where you met Matthew?"

"Yup. We were college sweethearts." She looks away, pretending she's busy.

"Wow." That's a long time.

Silence stretches between us, so I grab my phone. I make notes, saving the ideas I have and recipes I want to try. I have a feeling that Avery hasn't tried even a fraction of the ideas I've come up with. All of them are sure to bring in more business. I won't give her all my secrets, just the ones she'd be able to find in an online search if she were looking for ideas.

By the end of the day, Avery is yawning. I help her put away what's left over in the kitchen and take in the space back here. I hadn't had a chance to come see it earlier, but it's a decent-sized kitchen with plenty of storage space.

This location is everything I've been looking for—except for the stubborn woman by my side.

I feel like I missed the opportunity to have Sweet Delights in Emerald Bay since I wasn't ready to expand this far south when the old bakery was up for sale. By the time I heard the previous owners had retired, it was already purchased.

"What time do you start baking?" I look over at her.

"Four-thirty in the morning." She leans her hands on the island behind her and squeezes her eyes shut.

"I'll be here. Just giving you a head's up so you don't freak out."

"Why?" Her shoulders drop.

"We agreed to fifty-fifty. It's my turn to show you what I've got tomorrow." Excitement spreads through me like fireworks. I'm buzzing with the anticipation of getting in here and baking.

"Don't make me regret this." She sighs.

"Never." I salute her and laugh.

She looks at me unamused and shakes her head. "I'm gonna go."

"Right." We walk out of the bakery through the backdoor.

"See you tomorrow, Rudolph." I shift on my feet and look up at her apartment. Why is saying goodbye to this woman awkward? Last night felt the same. I didn't know how to separate, move along, go my own way.

She stands by the outdoor staircase that leads to her apartment, gripping the railing that's covered in Christmas lights. I learned last night that she lives above the bakery, which is helpful for getting to work on time.

"Bye, Grinch." I watch her climb the stairs before leaving.

Instead of heading home, I walk toward the bay. The palm trees that line the streets have lights wrapped around the trunks and huge, round ornaments hanging from the fronds. A sleigh with Santa and his reindeer brings life to the median near the bay, along with more decorated palm trees lining the area.

I walk toward the shore, removing my shoes and letting my feet sink into the cold sand. Wind creates a chill, but it's nothing compared to what I'm used to back in Denver.

The sound of the rolling waves is calming as I walk and think. If I can't get this deal, my dream of moving down to Emerald Bay is at risk. I could find a nearby town to open my Florida location, but I'd rather not have to. Having a bakery here has been on my bucket list since I opened my business. I remember the excitement on my grandmother's face when I told her about my dream. I can't let her down.

The sun has almost set; a sliver of orange lines the horizon. Combing a hand through my hair, I think of what I'm going to make tomorrow at the bakery. My plan is to make my usual recipes and introduce Sweet Delights through the desserts it's known for.

I'm banking on Avery loving what I have to offer, seeing it's a great fit, and surrendering to my plan. Okay, that sounds a bit like I want to take over the world, but my offer will be financially worth it to her.

You'd force her to give up her dream.

I feel sympathy for her. I know what it feels like to fight for something. My first few years in the business were brutal, but I've learned to separate emotions and business.

This is business. I need to remind myself of that.

8

AVERY

I'll admit that there is something sexy about a man in the kitchen. It's always been my kryptonite, so seeing Gabriel kneading dough in a T-shirt that does nothing to hide his defined chest is making me feel all kinds of hot—and the oven pre-heating is not to blame.

Taking a deep breath, I busy myself by washing the bowls he's not using anymore. If I don't look at him, it's like he's not here. I don't care how hot he is. He's not a possible match for me. Not that I'm looking to date. Absolutely not.

That's one Christmas miracle that will not happen.

"Can you hand me the cinnamon, please?" Gabriel's quiet voice breaks through my thoughts.

"Uh, yeah." I scurry toward the spices and grab the cinnamon, looking guilty as if he can read my thoughts. That would not be a good thing.

I place it on the counter in front of him and watch him work again, not admiring his arms flex with his movements. Not at all.

Liar.

"My cinnamon rolls are a favorite in every Sweet Delights store. You're going to love them." He smiles like a dazzling prince, but I'm not buying it.

It's true that he's been upfront about his visit, but something about this whole deal irks me. Like if he doesn't get what he wants, he'll find a way to take it, and I can't afford that.

"While you do that, I'm going to cut the leftover cupcakes from yesterday into small pieces for samples."

Gabriel arrived insisting we do samples today. Since I can't sell those cupcakes anymore, I figured I might as well try it.

"Great idea." He looks up at me with another wide smile before getting back to work.

The way he concentrates is impressive; his expression neutral and focused on his task. He doesn't get distracted. When I'm working, I sing and dance, look around, and think a million things at once. Sometimes I have to stop to write down a new recipe idea that hits me.

"Wanna turn up the volume?" He lifts his gaze.

"Really?" I lift my eyebrows and stare at him.

"Yeah." He nods eagerly. "I love this song."

"Wow, okay." I raise the volume to Taylor Swift's version of "Last Christmas."

Gabriel mouths the words, his body moving slightly. So much for his focused demeanor. I guess he's got a weak spot for Taylor Swift. I can't blame the guy. Her music speaks to my soul.

I plate the samples and take them out to the front of the store. Looking around the bakery, sadness fills me. I love this place—it's my home—but at what point do you face reality and accept what's being shown to you? The financial reports don't lie.

I hop on my feet, shaking my hands to get rid of the heavy feeling. Then, I turn on the Christmas display lights and move to the tree. I need something to make me happy, and Christmas decorations usually do the trick.

Gabriel's voice cracks on a high note heard all the way out here, and I cover my mouth and laugh. Tiptoeing toward the kitchen, I peek my head in and see him using the whisk as a microphone, going all out.

I lean against the entrance and cross my arms. The song comes to an end, and I clear my throat, eyebrows raised. Then, I slow-clap for his performance.

"Good, you didn't miss my show." He winks and places the whisk back on the counter, grabbing the sheet that already has the cinnamon rolls.

"If the store next door was open already, I have no doubt people would've heard you." I shake my head, walking into the kitchen.

I stand there idly, unsure of what to do with myself. I'm used to moving around, being in control of this part of my life.

I hate not being able to bake, but he said today was his day. I'm here as an observer. In my own business. What has my life become?

Gabriel chuckles and shrugs unapologetically. "The cinnamon rolls will be done fairly quickly, and then it's opening time." He cleans the counter, wiping every last bit of proof that it was used for prep work.

Gabriel made his famous cinnamon rolls (which my mouth is watering for, but I'll deny it all the way to my grave), his lemon pound cake (not excited about that), a chocolate roll cake that looks like a log, muffins, and donuts. None of it is decorated for Christmas, which is driving me crazy because this time of year is when I go all out on making my sweets reflect the season.

When I tried to sneak in my own recipe, he didn't let me, saying we have an agreement to uphold. I curse the day Matthew walked in here with his girlfriend, and I felt the need to prove I'd moved on.

I grab my phone and see a message from Lizzy.

Lizzy: I thought it was just rumors, but everyone is talking about you dating some new guy named Gabriel?????

Lizzy: Don't ignore me with this bombshell!

Lizzy: HELLO? Are you currently making out with him?

Lizzy: Damn I also heard Matthew's in town with his new girlfriend. Are you okay? Let's meet up today after work. I'll pass by the bakery.

Me: Hey sorry I was busy prepping for today. It's a rumor but it's complicated. I'll explain today when you come by.

Me: And yeah, I saw Matthew and met Jessy. It was a disaster and what caused the rumors. It's a conversation to have with a glass of wine.

Lizzy: Deal. Want me to tell Dani? She's asking me all sorts of questions. I'm surprised you haven't heard from her.

Me: Me too. I'll see you both later.

Lizzy: Ok!

I rub my forehead and slide my phone into my *Let's Get Baked* apron's wide pocket, excited about seeing my friends later. Between Dani's demanding job at the radio station and Lizzy teaching and spending time with her boyfriend, sometimes we don't get to see each other as often as I'd like, but they've been my biggest cheerleaders these past months.

"Ready to rock and roll?" Gabriel takes the cinnamon rolls out of the oven and drizzles them with glaze.

"Yeah." I sigh, walking out of the kitchen.

I unlock the door and flip over the *Open* sign. When I turn around, Gabriel is standing behind the counter with excitement. He's put on his jacket and his green Grinch apron. My eyes move to the display, and it looks nothing like what I'm used to. My heart breaks a bit, thinking this is the beginning of the end.

No. Don't let the negativity get to you. Everyone goes through bumps in the road.

Customers start to drop in, slowly and sparingly at first, but as soon as they see Gabriel behind the counter with me, their eyes spark with curiosity.

"You don't have your Christmas cookies today?" A customer says with furrowed brows. "I was hoping to buy some for my daughter."

"Not today, but I'll be sure to have them tomorrow," I respond, cutting my gaze to Gabriel.

"You should try my famous cinnamon rolls, though," he says charmingly.

"That would be great, thanks. I'll come by tomorrow for the cookies."

"Excellent." I smile.

"Christmas treats are a selling point." My voice rings with an *I-told-you-so* tone.

"I never said they weren't, but this is to show you that my recipes are long-lasting. What happens when the holidays are over, and people aren't forced to buy anything for co-workers, holiday parties, or school activities? This time of year is a strong one for bakeries, but your struggles go beyond that." His face is serious, yet his tone is sympathetic.

"Fine." There's nothing else to say because he's right.

"Hi!" Jessy strolls in, with Matthew lagging a few feet behind. I take a calming breath and smile. "Hello."

"Ohhh! You have lemon cake. I'll take a slice." Her eyes widen when she sees the loaf of cake in the display.

"Coming right up." Gabriel cuts her a slice and plates it.

"You work here now?" Matthew arches an eyebrow, looking between Gabriel and me.

"Just helping her out." He winks at me. "What kind of boyfriend would I be if I didn't support my girl?"

His words have a greater impact than he realizes since Matthew wasn't crazy about this idea when I first opened. His face hardens, but he instantly relaxes his features and wraps an arm around Jessy.

For the first time since I've met him, I can't get a read on Matthew. It seems as if Gabriel bothers him, although he's the one who fell out of love.

"Absolutely," he says.

"Do you want to try some?" Jessy holds a fork up to his lips, but he shakes his head.

"Your loss." She eats the bite, moaning at how delicious it is. "This is the best one I've tried, and I am a tough judge of lemon cake." She continues to eat.

"I'm glad you like it," Gabriel says with a proud grin.

"Yup. Me too." I fidget with my hands, moving a glass plate an inch forward and then to the left to keep busy.

"I'm so glad I came by today. We've been walking around town, seeing all the spots. Emerald Bay is so charming. And the beach is gorgeous. Too bad it's so cold." Jessy shivers.

"We have our Christmas festival this weekend, too. I'll have a stand with some sweets, so make sure you pass by."

Oh my, goodness. What are you doing, Avery? Inviting your ex and his new girlfriend to stop by your stand. You've lost your mind. Or you're just that desperate.

"I'm so excited about it! The Christmas tree at the boardwalk is gorgeous, and the town looks so pretty with all the decorations." Jessy's hand holding the fork waves all over the air as she talks.

"We should get going." Matthew steps in.

"Right. We have to go Christmas shopping. I wasn't sure what to get my in-laws, so Matthew is going to help me." She places the plate on the counter.

I blanch at her words, and my heart skips. *In-laws.* Searching her hand, I don't see an engagement ring, so it must be a way of speaking. It wasn't too long ago that I was shopping for them. Planning the holidays with them.

"Let's go." Matthew pays for the slice of cake and guides Jessy out of the bakery.

I blow out a breath, resting my hands behind me on the counter and bowing my head.

"Are you okay?" Gabriel's voice is soft.

"Fine," I grit.

"You don't have to pretend around me."

I snap my head up and stare at him. "If there's anyone I need to pretend the most with, it's you. You could use this to your advantage and make it another selling point to buy me out."

I snort humorlessly and walk to the kitchen. Sitting on a stool, I place my face in my hands and breathe evenly. I can survive this. I *am* surviving this.

9
AVERY

The day has passed at a slower pace than yesterday, but people have come in and bought some stuff. Some have even made special orders for the weekend since many people are already having holiday gatherings.

It's a relief. Not just for my bank account but for my mental health. Thankfully, I had a mental break last night with Lizzy and Dani. It was a much-needed girls' night where I was able to get them up to speed with what's going on.

I head into the kitchen to eat my lunch while Gabriel stays out front. One perk of having him here is that I can eat in peace.

Taking my hair down, I massage my scalp. These bangs aren't growing fast enough for my liking. Every time I see them in the mirror, I cringe.

"Whoa." Gabriel halts at the entrance of the kitchen, laughing. "What kind of *There's Something About Mary* situation is this?" He bends over, slapping his knee.

I scramble to twist my bangs, no doubt standing straight up from being slicked back all day. It's pointless, though.

"No, no. Please let me look at this." He walks toward me, brushing my bangs down.

"Stop being an ass. I had a meltdown and tried to cut bangs. I just wanted to look cute. Sorry, not everyone's life is perfect like yours."

"At least it wasn't a 2007 Britney-level meltdown," he quips. "And my life isn't perfect, but I make the best of what I have."

"Right." I snort in disbelief.

"I know all about struggles and fighting for what you want." He widens his stance, face turning hard.

"Then why are you trying to take away the sliver of happiness I have left?" I cross my arms, not giving a shit if my bangs make me look insane.

"I'm offering you money. A big payout. You'll be able to live comfortably for a while until you figure out your next step."

"This is my next step." I wave a hand around.

"Look, Avery, I'm not the bad guy here." He exhales in frustration and steps away. "For what it's worth, you look cute with crazy bangs or without them." He leaves me alone in the kitchen with the echo of his words.

"What in the hell?" I mutter to myself.

I fix my hair and eat my lunch before getting back to work. Damn scissors and early morning ideas. Never make decisions before coffee.

When I see Gabriel charming a customer, I freeze. *Does he just flirt with everyone?*

"Time for samples!" I interrupt their conversation. Then, I place a Santa hat on his head and push him out the door with the platter of cupcake chunks.

"Sorry about that. We have a strict schedule to adhere to." I finish ringing up the customer.

Meanwhile, Gabriel is dancing around outside with the platter and Santa hat, calling out, "Free samples! Try your favorite cupcake today!"

I wipe the counter as I watch him tell a few kids that he's one of Santa's elves offering treats. Then he calls out, "Ho, ho, ho," as people pass by, practically shoving the platter in their faces.

I laugh as I observe his antics. He's getting people to take samples, though. It's hard to tell if it's because of him or if it's the word "free" that pulls them in. No one turns down anything that's free.

He moves around, chatting with people and laughing with them. As angry as I was with him earlier, his attitude is contagious, and I smile.

"You've got quite the cheerleader out there." I look away from Gabriel and at the woman who's just walked in.

"Oh, yeah. How can I help you?"

"Any chance you're selling him?" She throws her thumb over her shoulder.

"Ha! Wouldn't that be great. Unfortunately, he's not for sale." I shrug apologetically. "But we do have some great donuts."

"Those do look good. I'll take one of the jelly-filled. This place is really cute."

"You're not from Emerald Bay, right?"

"No." She laughs. "Is it obvious? I'm here for Christmas, visiting extended family."

"Are you liking the town so far?" It's easier to talk to a stranger who is oblivious to the small-town rumors.

"It's adorable. I'm from South Florida and love the change in atmosphere and pace."

"I can imagine." I slide her donut into a bag and ring her up.

"Thanks," she says. "And keep the elf. He clearly knows how to have fun."

"He's not..." I stop myself because it's too complicated to explain, and I don't need word getting around to Matthew that

Gabriel isn't anything to me. "I will. Have a nice day and thanks for stopping by."

"You're welcome." She leaves, laughing at Gabriel when he bows in exaggeration.

I shake my head and chuckle.

"Phew, they tore those samples from me. See what I mean?" He takes off the hat and wipes his brow.

"Now we need those people to come in and buy. Only a couple did."

"Patience, Young Grasshopper. They will." He's so confident that I roll my eyes.

"I hear I just missed a great show." Mrs. Barber storms in. I'm friends with her son, Luke, and she's been a sweetheart to me this entire time.

"Mrs. Barber." Gabriel smiles and walks over to her.

"Hi, dear, how are you? Word around town is that you're Santa's elf?" She smiles.

"At your service." He bows again.

"That's what I like to hear because I'm in a pickle." She clutches her hands and frowns.

"I'll do anything to help. What's going on?"

"We have the Christmas festival on Saturday, as I'm sure you've heard, and my elf is sick."

"I'm sorry?" Gabriel's eyes widen.

"Not a real elf, the man playing the part of Santa's elf. Would you mind stepping in and acting the part?" She gives him a wide smile.

"Sure. Well, that's if Avery doesn't need help at her stand."

"Oh, please." I wave him off. "You'll help me during the gingerbread house decorating class in the morning and then, by all means, give the people what they want."

"Thank you, honey." She looks at me.

"Anything I can do for the town, you know I will," I tell her.

"You'll just have to help bring the kids over to our Santa for pictures. It's pretty simple and won't take all night."

"I can do that." He nods confidently, but I am just waiting to see him in that costume.

"Oh, are those your cinnamon rolls?" She tilts her head toward Gabriel.

"Yup. That's the last one, too."

"I'll take it." She looks over at me and squeezes his arm. "They're my favorite."

Gabriel's face lights up. When his eyes collide with mine, instead of holding an air of superiority, I see genuine pride. I know that feeling. It's the same one that fills me when a customer gushes over my creations. Knowing that you can make people feel so happy with what you bake is so fulfilling.

"You two are close," I say once Mrs. Barber leaves.

"We're neighbors. I'm friends with Luke, and my grandparents were close to the Barbers. They helped a lot once they got older, and I'll always be grateful to them for that." He grabs the rectangular platter the cinnamon rolls were on and goes to the kitchen.

Maybe I underestimated Gabriel. He knows people in town, and one by one, he seems to be winning them over. A black cloud settles over me because the more they love him, the quicker they'll get over me.

With that thought, I rush to the kitchen and stare at him.

"The deal's off," I announce.

"What?" He looks over at me from the sink.

"Our agreement. I changed my mind. You can tell people I lied." *What are you doing, Avery?*

I ignore my conscience and don't backtrack.

"No."

"What?" I stare at him.

"I said no." He walks toward me like a lion inching toward his prey.

I swallow thickly and watch him move, ready for his attack. I'm not sure I'm a match for him, but I'll defend myself until the death.

"I won't sell to you." I cross my arms.

Gabriel smirks, standing toe-to-toe with me. He tilts his head, danger screaming inside of me. His fingers push a stray strand behind my ear. It's a thin piece of hair, so I'm not sure why he's even doing that, but it makes my heart speed up as his fingers barely brush the shell of my ear.

"We made a deal, and I take verbal agreements seriously." His eyes stare into mine, and I'm tempted to get lost in the sea green color that reminds me of a deep forest.

Right on cue, "All I Want for Christmas Is You" starts playing. A slow smile spreads on his face, framed by his stubble. If this were a movie, it'd start snowing outside. An anomaly in Florida.

"Hello?" A voice calls out, and I snap out of the hypnotizing energy and step away.

Gabriel breathes out, scrubbing a hand across his jaw.

"We stick to our agreement until the end of next week. If you don't think it's your best option, then we part ways. But, if you see that the best solution for all of us is selling to me, we draw up a contract."

How can he go from that intense moment to business talk? I'm still trying to get my heart to slow down and my goosebumps to disappear. Thank goodness I'm wearing a sweater, so he can't see the effect he had on me.

I nod and walk out to the bakery to see who's there. I halt when I see Emma standing by the counter. Her eyes widen when Gabriel comes out behind me.

"Hi, Emma." I feel like I'm depleted of energy.

"Hi, I was hoping to come by and order a cake for Christmas Eve." She doesn't take her eyes off Gabriel.

"Sorry, he can't be made into a cake," I say, no longer caring about the consequences.

"I'm sorry?" Her eyes widen toward me.

"You keep looking at him."

"I heard you were seeing someone, but I thought it was just a rumor. Seems as if what people are saying is true."

"My personal life is no longer your business." I cross my arms, exhausted from being the nice person that everyone walks over or quickly forgets. Maybe if I were more assertive, they'd take me seriously.

I sense Gabriel a few feet away, observing the situation.

"You're right. I'm sorry, but I'm happy you're happy."

"Thanks. What kind of cake would you like?" I grab my notepad.

"Oh, right. I love your red velvet cake. I'd need it for fifteen people." That information is pointless. I know how many people she has for Christmas each year. The count would only change if my parents were in town.

I take note. "Would you like any special decorating?"

"Yes, the crushed candy cane on top."

I add the details to the order.

"Sounds good. I'll need to take a deposit now."

"Oh." Her lips purse.

"Protocol." I smile.

"I see. Of course." I've never charged her for anything, so it doesn't surprise me she has no idea how I work.

I charge her for half the cake as security that she'll pick it up. I can't risk losing any more money and being stuck with a cake I may not be able to sell to someone else.

"I'll pick it up the morning of the twenty-fourth."

"Excellent. I'll be open until four that day."

"Perfect. Thank you."

"You're welcome." I watch her go.

Maybe staying in the town where Matthew's from wasn't the smartest decision.

"Was that *Matty's* mom?"

I close my eyes and chuckle. "Yeah." I look at Gabriel.

"They look alike."

"Thanks for the laugh. He actually hates that nickname."

"I could tell by the way he grimaced each time Jessy used it. Are you okay?"

"I'm fine." I reposition the trays and platters in the display to use up this antsy feeling.

Gabriel grabs my shoulders and stops me. "Sorry for being so rough back there, but I'm not backing down."

"Okay." I stare at his apron-covered chest. "We have work to do if you think you're going to convince me. A few basic recipes won't do the trick."

"Basic?" His eyebrows shoot up. "Game on, Rudolph." He pushes up the sleeves of his jacket and smirks like the Grinch himself.

10
GABRIEL

Avery and I have spent the last couple of days arguing about our different opinions, like if it's necessary to give out samples every day. My answer is yes.

I've also been fighting my growing attraction to her. I can't help it when she's singing along to a song without realizing it, swaying to the beat. Her hips move in a sensual way that makes me swallow thickly. Yesterday, I almost grabbed her hand and danced with her. Thankfully, someone walked in before I could make a fool of myself.

"We need this to be perfect. Have you put your batch in the oven already? Grinch!" She shouts, arms on her hips.

"It's going great." I nod.

Today's the gingerbread house decorating class, and she's a nervous wreck. We've split the task, each of us focusing on certain parts of the house that the kids will assemble. I'm working on the rectangular slabs for the roof and side walls, and she's working on the triangular walls.

Avery is old school and hand-cuts the pieces with a template she has. I suggested she should get cutters, and that got me a death stare.

She's got it down to a science, which is impressive. I had to admit that I'd never made a gingerbread house, which made Avery smile smugly.

"Can you watch the ones in the oven? I'm going to set up the tables outside."

"Yeah." I focus on cutting the dough into the right sizes using her template and humming to the music.

She always has it louder while she bakes in the mornings, and it's a nice distraction that makes the early morning pass by faster. It's like you work to the upbeat rhythm.

"Can you help me a sec?" Avery calls out.

"Be right there." I finish off this piece and wash my hands.

"Do you think that I should put this table parallel to this one or make a T shape?"

I smile at her without responding. Avery stares at me impatiently.

"What?" She lifts her hands in the air.

"I like that you're asking my opinion."

She rolls her eyes and pushes a chair in. "It's just a second opinion. I'd ask anyone. So? What do you think?"

"I'd leave them parallel. It leaves more room to move around." I walk toward the tables.

"I hope everyone shows up." She lets out a long exhale, wiping her palms on her apron. Today's apron has three gnomes with the wording: *Baking with my Gnomies*.

"They will." I hold her shoulders and force her to look at me. "It will be great." I can't help but encourage her. The feeling of sympathy has been growing the more I watch her work.

"What's that smell?" She sniffs, and I take a deep inhale. "The cookies!" She runs toward the kitchen, but she steps on a napkin and falls. I try to reach for her, but it's too late.

Avery groans on the floor, holding her arm.

"Are you okay? Don't move yet." I kneel beside her, softly touching her arm.

"Forget me. Go take out the cookies."

"You're hurt."

"Who cares. Go!" She sits up, stress lining her face and tears swimming in her eyes. "Please," she pleads.

I nod, standing and doing as she asks. If she's embarrassed, I don't want her to feel worse, but I also don't like leaving her there.

Smoke puffs out of the oven when I walk into the kitchen, and I curse. Throwing the door open, I grab oven mitts and slide out the cookie sheet. No doubt they're like charcoal.

"Shit, shit, shit," I mumble. The cookie sheet lands on the island with a loud bang, causing the cookies to crack. "Wonderful." I shake my head.

"Fuck."

I look at Avery with a frown. "Sorry. I got caught up out there helping you and forgot about them."

"This can't be happening." She presses the heels of her palms into her eyes.

I round the island and grab her wrists, pulling her hands down.

"Did you do this on purpose?" She narrows her eyes. "A way of sabotaging me."

"Of course not. I've never had to cheat to win." My jaw ticks. I can't believe she'd think that. "We'll fix this. I'll pay for the damaged cookies and get the amount we need done." I pull her into a hug, breaking every rule in this professional agreement because seeing her distraught is killing me.

Avery sniffs and pushes off my chest.

"We have less than an hour."

"Never underestimate the Gabriel Hill Super Speed." I extend my arms. "I'm Santa's elf, so I've got some magic to sprinkle."

She looks at me unimpressed, her lips pinched together, but I won't let that deter me.

"Come on." I grab her arm. "Actually, are you sure you're okay?"

"Yup, permanently bruised ego, remember?"

"Let's get to work, Rudolph."

While she makes the dough, I find something that will form the shapes faster than hand cutting. Using the templates, I fit the two sizes into different containers she has and find some that are close in size for both the walls and roof.

"This could work as a cutter for the rectangles we need." I hold up the containers. "And I actually think we could use this one for the front and back as well, and we'd just need to cut the corners to make the triangle shape."

Avery stares at me while I wait for a reaction.

"I was aiming for a wide smile, excitement, maybe a hug."

"That could work. At this rate, I'm so exhausted trying to make this bakery work that I have to question if this is a sign." She tosses her head back. "Maybe I should just sell to you and leave town."

"Hey, now, you're a fighter. You can't just give up."

"Isn't that what you want?" She shrugs.

"I like the challenge." I lift a shoulder. "Besides, I don't want you to make a hasty decision when you're feeling down and then regret it."

Avery rolls her eyes and grabs one of the containers. I should take advantage of this opportunity, but one thing I've learned about her is that she loves this place. It wouldn't be a fair win.

We rush to work efficiently, Avery rolling out the dough while I cut the shapes and place them in the oven. No burning them this time. I'll stand by the oven door if necessary.

"Why did you want to run your own bakery?" I ask her while I work.

"I've loved baking since I can remember. It always made me happy. I love mixing ingredients, trying different flavors that may not be the norm." She looks over at me, a strand of her crooked bangs falling onto her forehead. The piece doesn't even reach her eyebrow.

"I get that. Isn't it amazing to come up with something people love so much? Something that makes them smile."

"Yes." She stands, stretching her back. "I love to see people's reactions, knowing that I had a hand in making them happy, satisfied."

I wouldn't mind knowing how she can satisfy me.

My eyes drop to her lips when she says satisfied, but I quickly lift them to her eyes.

"Yeah." I place the slabs of cookie on the baking sheet and check on the ones in the oven. "These are ready." I remove them and add two more trays.

I'd love to say that two trays are all we need, but these pieces are big, and only a few fit on one tray. I need to be sure we catch up and get them all done in the next forty minutes before she needs to open.

The workshop isn't until eleven, but I don't want her to be worried while serving customers. Somehow I've started to care about how Avery feels, and it's difficult to not want to make her smile.

"Oh, sorry." Avery moves to one side at the same time as me.

"Great minds," I joke and move to the left, but she mimics me. "Want to dance?" I hold my hand out.

"What?"

"A dance." I grab her hand and wrap my arm around her waist, spinning us in half a circle until we're both on the side we wanted to go to.

"That works." She smiles.

"At your service."

"The Grinch's heart didn't turn kind until the end of the movie."

"His heart grew, not turned kind."

"Potato, potahto." She shrugs, grabbing some flour to sprinkle on the countertop.

I laugh and focus on the rectangles I need to cut. When we both reach for a spatula, our fingers brush, and I look over at her. She shivers, and I smile.

"Go ahead," I tell her.

"Thanks."

"You know, I think you have what it takes to run a place like this."

"Geez, thanks. I've been doing it for a few years."

"So is the divorce the true blame? I thought that was an exaggeration, and you weren't managing it well." I turn to face her.

"Of course I'm managing it well, but Matthew's a local, and I'm not. His family is popular in town. When it came down to it, people took sides even though there was no competition. He moved and didn't want me to go with him." She rolls her eyes, pressing her lips into a straight line.

"He's an idiot," I mutter.

"Right." Avery tilts her head and stares at me. "Apparently, he wasn't happy. Whatever, I'm mostly over it, but the idea of a failed marriage weighs heavily on me. I was blindsided, though, and a surprise divorce makes you question your relationship even months later."

"I'm not blaming you for that." I squeeze her hand, and she freezes, looking at me with furrowed eyebrows.

"Sorry. Let's finish up here." My heart is racing.

I want to comfort her. I want to get to know her better; like why did she cut her bangs instead of going to the salon? I want to know what makes her tick.

I smirk to myself. I have a feeling I already know the answer to that, and it's me. I like that I get such a reaction out of her.

11

AVERY

I SMILE AS PEOPLE start to trickle in for the decorating class. I didn't think we'd make it happen, but I have to give Gabriel credit for working as a team. I left it as open time slots for two hours since it's not a structured workshop, and I'll be assisting throughout.

My heart soars as a few kids talk excitedly, dressed in Santa hats and looking around the bakery in awe. One little girl giggles when she sees a mischievous elf figure hanging upside down from the top of the tree.

"Welcome! Each spot has the kits already set. I'll help guide you in creating your structure, but the decorating is all up to your imagination." I smile at the few kids and motion for them to sit at the table.

I explain how to pipe the board they're using as a base with the size of the house and how to assemble it with the frosting.

Another child walks in, and I let the ones who have started working continue while I greet him. As I'm helping him settle, I lift my gaze at the newcomers and frown.

Jessy and Matthew.

I swear he's come in here more times this week than he had in the last year of our marriage. Maybe that was a clue something wasn't right. I need to stop overanalyzing our marriage and accept that it's over and done with. There's no point in finding what's broken if there's nothing to fix.

"This is so cute." Jessy claps her hands. "Is it for kids only, or can we join?"

"Of course, you can join." I nod and wave them in.

People are staring with amused curiosity. I'm sure they're loving this. *Come in and enjoy the hot mess that is my life. Front row seats and all.*

"Great," she exclaims and drags Matthew to a chair.

"Oh, hey." Gabriel walks out of the kitchen, wiping his hands on a towel. "You guys are going to make a house? That's great. Perfect for Christmas memories." He winks at me. "We're going to make ours tonight, right?"

He's really laying it on thick today.

"Yup." I bite my lips to stop myself from saying a snarky remark.

We focus on the class, and Gabriel helps in between customers. It's nice having some help in the bakery; for once, everything isn't falling on my shoulders.

"Hi." Lizzy walks in and pauses, eyes widening. "Well, I think I've walked into an alternate universe." She looks outside and back in. "Nope, this seems to be reality."

"Oh, it is my reality," I tell her.

"So, that's the hottie pretending to be your boyfriend so you can agree to sell him your bakery?"

"My Grinch, yes." I sigh and look at him talking to the kids and helping them.

"At least he's hot."

I look at her and close my eyes. "Don't remind me."

She laughs and wraps an arm around my shoulders. "Everything will be okay. It looks like you've got some kids here."

"Yeah, but I was counting on more. At least another ten to fifteen kids." I frown, staring at the empty spots.

"Maybe they'll come by later."

"Who knows. What are you up to? Where's Sean?" I'm surprised to see her here without her boyfriend.

"Ugh. We broke up."

"What? When?" I saw her the other day, and she didn't mention anything.

"Last night. I couldn't take it anymore. He kept wanting me to quit my job and stay home. Then he dropped hints that he expected dinner to be ready when he got home from work and wouldn't help me around the house. If this was a preview of what living with him would be like, then I'm not having it." She rolls her eyes.

"I'm sorry to hear that."

"It sucks, but I'm not a Susie Homemaker. I'm glad I realized it now before..." She bites her lips. "Sorry! I didn't mean to offend you."

"You didn't offend me." I laugh. "I'm glad you realized it earlier on in your relationship as well. Maybe you'll meet a hunk this coming year." I waggle my eyebrows.

"No." She crosses her arms. "The next man I meet better prove he's different. I've kissed too many toads."

Laughing, I ask, "Want to make a house? On me."

"Sure, but I'm paying. I need to get in the Christmas spirit again. I'm not sure what to do with the gift I got him. He would probably hate it and criticize it." Her lips snarl. "Yes, focus on anger instead of hurt." She nods to herself.

"Return the gift," I say.

"Yeah." She sighs, sitting across from Matthew and Jessy. "Hey." She smiles at them and then focuses on her gingerbread house.

"Is that a friend?" Gabriel whispers in my ear. I ignore the shiver that runs down my spine when his breath hits my skin.

"Yeah. Lizzy."

"Cool. So what do you think? Happy with the turnout so far?"

"Honestly?" I turn to look at him.

"Of course."

"No. I was expecting more than double this amount." I look over at the people here. "I'm grateful for those that did come, though."

"It's not too late. There's still an hour to go." He smiles, squeezing my arm. "I'll be back." He walks into the kitchen and returns with a Christmas hat.

Instead of coming back to the tables, he goes outside and claps his hands.

"Come in and join us. Get in the Christmas spirit early by making your own gingerbread house! All are welcome. Holiday fun isn't just for children." He waves the hat in the air, and I shake my head, smiling.

Gabriel dances and laughs with people as they walk by, and I can't help but look at him through the window. He's singing "Jingle Bells" off-beat, not a care that he looks like a fool. He's doing this for me. My smile widens as warmth seeps through me.

"You look happy." I startle and look to the right to see Matthew standing beside me.

"Oh, yeah. Of course. So do you." I point to Jessy.

"She's great." He stands beside me with his hands in his pockets. "I'm glad you're happy, Ave."

"Uh, huh." I avoid his eyes because this isn't my true life, but today Gabriel is making me feel differently, and I don't know what to make of it.

When someone comes in for the class, Gabriel looks at me and winks. Shaking my head, I can't hide my smile.

"Excuse me," I tell Matthew.

I welcome the newcomer and get them started. The rest of the children are already decorating the outside with jellybeans, sprinkles, and candy canes.

Gabriel continues to attract customers, and soon I have filled five more spots. I don't even know how to thank him or why he's doing this, but I appreciate it.

By the time I finish for the day, I'm exhausted and rushing to clean up so I can set up my stand for the Christmas festival. Only I would schedule two big events on the same day, but it was the best day for the gingerbread house workshop since kids are already out of school and the house will last them until closer to Christmas. Thankfully, everyone loved the class.

"I can help you set up at the stand before changing into costume," Gabriel offers.

"Um, that'd be great, actually. The stand is set already, but I need to decorate and bring all the desserts."

Besides the gingerbread houses and everything else I needed to have for the bakery, I made three types of treats for the festival—spiced donuts, chocolate cake squares with cream cheese frosting and crushed candy canes on top, and vanilla cupcakes with the frosting like a Christmas tree. *Thank you, mini ice cream cones, for the shape.*

"Great, put me to work, Rudolph."

"Can you package the cake squares while I change?" My jeans and sweater are stained with frosting, flour, and something I'm hoping is just butter. So much for wearing an apron.

"Of course." He moves around the kitchen while I race upstairs to my apartment.

Grabbing the outfit I left lying on my bed, I take the fastest shower known to mankind and fix my hair. I release the braid I had earlier and curl it with my wand. Then I re-twist my bangs, pin them back, and swipe a bit of red lipstick on.

I throw on the black skirt and red sweater, zip up my ankle boots, and race back downstairs.

"Oh, I'm gonna use this." I grab the Christmas hat and realize it faintly smells of Gabriel's cologne. The woodsy scent makes me feel like I'm in a pine field.

Great, his scent is going to haunt me all evening. As if I need another reason to think about the man who's slowly winning my heart.

"Wow," Gabriel breathes out. "You look great."

"Oh." I look down at my outfit. "Thanks."

He nods, taking me in. His eyes blaze a trail up and down my body while I awkwardly shift on my feet. What is going on with us today? Maybe the holiday spirit has gone to our heads.

"Ready to go?" I ask, grabbing the large tote with all the decorations.

"Yeah, of course." He nods, grabbing the transporting containers with the desserts.

We walk through town toward the boardwalk where the festival is held each year.

"Thanks for all your help today. I didn't tell you earlier, but I appreciate that you went outside and brought in some new customers." I focus on the path before me, afraid that if I look at him, he'll see through my cracked armor.

"You don't need to thank me."

"I do. You could've sabotaged the event, made me look worse than I already do, and benefitted from it."

"I already told you that that's not how I play." He pauses, causing me to stop as well. His face is illuminated by the string lights wrapped around a lamppost.

Our eyes catch, intensity flowing through us. I don't know what's happening, but I want to lean in and kiss him. I want to feel his strong arms wrapped around me and roaming up and down my body.

"Hello, Avery. Are you going to the festival?"

"Mrs. Daniels, hi. Yes, we are. I mean, I am. I mean, we. Yes." Gabriel snickers across from me.

"We'll be there," he says confidently. "I'll be the elf, so keep an eye out for me, and don't forget to buy a treat."

"Of course. I wouldn't miss it for the world. I love Avery's desserts." She eyes us with a spark, and I swear I see the wheels turning in her mind.

"See you there, then." Gabriel waves her off and turns to me. "You're so not cool."

"I never claimed to be, Grinch." I walk in front of him, heading to the stand so that I make it on time.

Whatever that was a moment ago cannot happen again. He is not my boyfriend or my crush. He's my Grinch.

12
AVERY

"I need to look for Mrs. Barber to get my outfit. You're good here?" Gabriel looks at me as I add a set of gnomes to the wooden stand.

I love that our town doesn't just have plain tables for vendors. These are like something I'd imagine in Europe, small red roofs and all. String lights circle around each post that holds the roof, and a wreath hangs in front of the main platform.

"I'm great. Go on and do your job." I smile at him, way too excited to see this play out.

"See you later, Rudolph."

I watch him walk away—saunter is more like it—and greet a few people in town.

Excitement buzzes in the air as people begin to crowd the boardwalk. Friends gather, families talk, and children laugh. The magic of Christmas is palpable, and I can't help but get caught up in it. For one night, I want to enjoy the Christmas spirit and leave stress and worries to the side.

Other stands are set up all around the boardwalk selling holiday gifts, coffee, and hot cocoa. The air is filled with the salty smell of the ocean, making Christmas here unique.

The huge Christmas tree is full of ornaments, from Christmas balls to stars to large bows. It's majestic, and I'm sure it'll look even more beautiful once the lights are on.

"Hey." Lizzy walks up to me with a smile.

"Hi, did you have fun this morning? Sorry I couldn't talk to you before you left."

"No worries. I know you were busy, which is great." She squeezes my arm.

"Yeah, but I worry about what will happen after the holidays. Everyone is coming in to be nosy about Gabriel." I take a deep breath.

"Everything will work out. You're still set on not selling, right?"

I shake my head but frown. "Maybe it's the best option. If not now, I might have to close months down the line when supporting my business and myself with half the income isn't enough, but I can give myself until after the summer and hope tourism sparks a new wave of interest."

"Have faith." Lizzy smiles.

"Yeah. Is Dani DJing today?" She usually loves working events like this.

"No, but she should be coming to see us soon. I'll help you finish here." Lizzy moves around the stand and grabs the cupcakes, setting them on the tiered stand I brought.

We finish plating what's left of the sweets and then high-five each other. I love my friends. I can't imagine not living here anymore. Minnesota is where I'm from, but Emerald Bay has become my home.

"Hey, hey." Dani walks over to us with a grin. "This looks amazing. I want one of everything." She leans forward to look at my desserts.

Laughing, I shove her away. Don't get your breath on them; I need to sell out tonight.

"You've got it, Ave." Dani gives me a thumbs up.

A few people stop by to say hello and get something to eat. I'm grateful for those who have remained loyal and supportive. Without those people in town, I probably would've packed my bags and fled long before now.

"What in the..." Dani's surprised tone interrupts me. Then, she bends over, laughing.

I look up, and my eyes widen. I snort, covering my mouth and biting my lips, but I can't control the guffaw that roars out of me.

Gabriel is standing a few feet away with Mrs. Barber. He looks unimpressed as she panics and waves her hands in the air. When he lifts his gaze and locks with mine, I walk toward him.

"Well, well, well... This is so fitting." I choke back a laugh, trying and failing to maintain a serious expression.

I look him up and down. He's no elf. He's dressed as Grinch. Green tights, green hairy hands, and a Santa coat that has a hairy green hoody.

"Is this my Christmas miracle?" I smirk.

"You wish." He scratches his jaw. "The costumes got mixed up somehow."

"It's fine. It's okay. You can still help." Mrs. Barber's eyes are wide with panic, and I feel so bad for her. "We don't have time to change the costumes. We're starting in ten minutes. We'll swap roles and say this is the year that Santa and Grinch teamed up to make the best Christmas." She looks at me as if she's silently asking if it's a believable story.

"That works." I offer a sympathetic smile. I know all about things not going according to plan.

"Thanks. I'm going to tell Santa." Mrs. Barber leaves us alone.

"At least it's long enough to cover your junk." I point to the long coat that hits the top of his thighs.

He arches a brow. "Barely."

I swallow thickly, my neck heating, but I won't fall into that trap.

"Just for you, Rudolph. Look all you want. By the way, I think they need you up by Santa's sleigh." He taps my nose.

"Jerk." I roll my eyes.

"I can't tell if this is part of their game or real." I hear Lizzy tell Dani, and I swear she's purposely talking loud enough for Gabriel to hear her.

"I think it's real, and boy is it hot."

"Thanks, ladies." Gabriel winks.

"Don't scare the children," I say, ignoring the commentary.

This is way too fun. I'm going to need a picture.

Whoa... You do not need any pictures of Gabriel. You don't need to save any memories.

"Kids love me."

"Good luck."

"Luck's always on my side." He gives me a lopsided smile and walks toward Santa.

I've got a clear view of the event since Santa's sleigh for pictures is across from my stand. Laughing to myself, I return to my friends and my stand.

"You know what I think?" Dani lifts her brows. "You two would make a great *real* couple," she says without waiting for my response.

"We wouldn't." I take a deep breath. "He's kind of like the enemy."

"But he isn't because he's been forthcoming, and he's giving you an option," Lizzy says level-headedly.

"He's not even from here." I throw a hand in the air.

"Ah, that has a solution, though." Dani waggles her eyebrows.

"This is ridiculous. Gabriel and I are not a couple." I move behind the stand.

"Really?" Matthew saunters over to us.

Ugh.

"What?" I lift my brows, pretending I have no idea what he's talking about.

"You and Gabriel aren't a real thing?" He lifts his brows.

"Oh, of course, we are. We were talking about those couples that always match. We're not that kind of couple. It kinda irks me when people do that." I scrunch up my nose.

Matthew tilts his head right as Jessy skips up to us, and Dani slaps the top of the stand, laughing hysterically.

"Sorry, sorry," she says between hiccups. "I'm gonna…" She abandons ship, walking away while her entire body rocks with laughter.

Lizzy snorts beside me in an attempt to hold in her laugh, but it's useless.

Jessy and Matthew are in matching ugly sweaters, each complete with a reindeer head and lights that actually light up.

"I, uh."

"Right." Matthew's jaw ticks.

I guess people do change in relationships because I never once saw Matthew in an ugly sweater, but seeing him match with Jessy is the icing on the cake.

"Your booth is so cute," Jessy says, oblivious to the awkward tension.

"Thanks." I look at the platters and trays, arranging them so I can avoid Matthew's eyes.

I hope he believed my excuse. The last thing I need is for him to think that I lied about dating Gabriel and let that get to his head.

"Ho, ho, ho," Santa's voice booms, and we all turn to look before Jessy and Matthew leave us.

Gabriel stands beside him, looking confident, until the first kid stares at him and cries. He deflates, and I feel bad for him. I may have made fun of him, but he was actually excited about this role.

Another child tells him he's not an elf before walking straight to Santa without Gabriel's help. His shoulders slump each time a child doesn't want anything to do with him.

Unable to take it, I ask Lizzy if she can manage the stand for a moment. Her smile widens as she agrees.

I walk over to the side where Santa is and smile at the children in line.

"Have you met my friend?" I ask them, reaching out for Gabriel's arm. "He's great and has an amazing friendship with Santa." Gabriel looks at me with a grateful smile.

"He's not an elf, though." One boy crosses his arms.

"He's better than an elf. He's the Grinch, and now that his heart is huge, he and Santa work together to make Christmas the best." My voice rings with awe as I make up this story.

"Really?" A girl's eyes widen.

"Do you go on the sleigh with Santa?" she asks Gabriel.

"Nope, I stay at the North Pole with Mrs. Claus and make sure everything runs smoothly."

"Wow!" The girl gasps. "So, can I also tell you what I want?"

"Of course. Santa and I are a team."

Gabriel then looks over at me with a wink. After all the help today, I couldn't let him fail at this event—even if I did make fun of his outfit.

"That was nice of you." Lizzy arches her eyebrow when I return to the stand.

"I owed him one." I shrug.

"Right." Her smile is full of mischief, but I let it go.

I'm not sure what I'm feeling right now. I should keep my distance, yet there's a pull toward him that makes me hyper-aware when he's near. I can't let the Grinch steal my heart, though.

13
GABRIEL

I need to thank Avery. She saved me back there when the kids started calling me out. It's not my fault that the costumes got mixed up, but it made me feel so out of place.

As soon as I took the costume out of the bag, I knew it was wrong, but I had no other choice than to put it on and show Mrs. Barber. I couldn't bail on her after promising to help.

I sure as hell didn't expect the kids to gang up on me, though. The Grinch could be kind. At the end of the story, he becomes a good guy.

Avery swept in when I least expected it, and it made me want to grab her and kiss her.

The mayor interrupts the festivities to welcome everyone and wish us all a wonderful holiday season, quieting the entire crowd, and we take a break from the pictures.

I take advantage of the pause to look behind me, where Avery remains by her stand. She's smiling widely, looking like pure happiness. I like seeing her like this instead of the stressed woman afraid of losing that last bit of hope in her life.

I should back off this deal, but then it means I have to go home. For some reason, I'm not ready.

Actually, I know the reason, and it's the woman with the crooked bangs and the smile of an angel. If I take this deal off the table, I won't be able to spend more time with her. I refuse to lose the opportunity.

As the mayor finishes off his Christmas speech, an uproar of excitement fills the air as everyone breaks away in groups and begins talking again. Music plays from the DJ station, a combination of classics, pop songs, and country songs.

"Back to work," Santa says in a deep voice.

While I work as a dutiful helper, my eyes move to Avery. I watch her as she sells sweets and talks to friends and acquaintances. Her face lights up each time someone new stops by her stand, and I'm glad to see people paying her attention and support.

Her eyes find mine amongst the crowd, and I smile. She rolls her eyes, but I see the smile playing on her lips. She's enjoying this as much as I am.

"Hi." A small hand tugs my fingers.

"Hi." I bend down to look at the little girl who can't be more than five.

"Are you really the *good* Grinch?" Her brows furrow as if I'm really here to ruin Christmas.

"I am." I smile. "My heart's huge and full of love and Christmas spirit. Want to tell me what you want for Christmas?"

"Oh, sure." She swings her leg back and forth for a second as if contemplating how close she can get to me and then leans in. "I want a stuffed unicorn, a big piano on the floor so I can step on it and make music, and makeup."

"Makeup?"

"Yeah, but the toy kind. My mom said I can't ask for the real thing." The girl frowns, and I chuckle.

"I'll add those things to the list. Ready for a picture with Santa?"

"Can I get one with you first?" Her round eyes, full of hope, are impossible to turn down.

"Of course." I smile at her mom, holding a phone, and then guide the girl toward Santa and almost trip over these huge shoe covers that curl up at the end.

I steady myself and look around, embarrassed when some kids laugh. Shaking it off, I bow and laugh along with them.

There's no better remedy than laughing at yourself. It's something I learned through a few stumbles in life.

Once we finish, I walk to Avery's stand to see how things are going. I'm happy to see she's sold most of her inventory.

"Looks like you're doing great."

"Yeah. People have stopped by, even those who haven't come into the store in a while. I'm glad this event opened a more laidback opportunity for people to purchase from me." She exhales and grabs her hair, twirling it and then draping it over her shoulder.

"I'm happy to hear that." I shift on my feet and look out at the crowd before returning my gaze to her. "Thanks for helping me earlier. I didn't expect kids to be so anti-Grinch."

"Well, you did try to ruin Christmas." One side of her lips lifts in a smile.

"Not me, the character. I'm a fan of Christmas." It's the best time of year. I don't know how anyone could hate it.

"Did you think this time of year was right to come down here and try to buy my bakery?" She crosses her arms, looking stern.

"It was the time I had to make the trip. It's not personal." Although, I wouldn't mind getting personal with her in other ways. If I voiced that, she'd probably kick me in the jewels.

Instead of responding, I see her eyes cut to the side and back to me as she chews on her bottom lip.

"What's going on?"

"Nothing." She answers way too quickly.

"Avery?" I cross my arms.

"I cannot take you seriously in this costume." She snickers, shaking her head.

I hold back my response when someone else comes to buy a chocolate cake square, but I watch her interact with the customer. Avery exudes confidence when she's in her element, and I enjoy being a silent observer.

Her eyes once again move away from the stand, and I notice that Matthew is eyeing us with scrutiny. I shrug it off and get back to Avery.

"You're jittery."

"I'm not," she argues, but her fingers wring together as she looks behind me.

In a split second, her hands are gripping the front of my costume and pulling me to her. I'm surprised when her lips press against mine. We both freeze, eyes wide, and our mouths pressed together in a very awkward kiss.

Then I do what any sane man in my situation would do. I wrap my arm around her waist and kiss her with the unadulterated desire I've been trying to fight off the last few days.

Her lips warm against mine, and the tip of her cold nose soothes my heated cheeks. I keep my hold on her tight as I explore her mouth, kissing her without any reservations.

Our tongues meet, and the idea that she's right there with me makes my body react to her. My heart accelerates as her other arm comes around my neck. If I could drag her away and show her how she makes me feel, I would.

Avery's soft moan fuels me, and I deepen the kiss. Every thought evaporates from my mind. She's all I can think about, all I can smell, all I can taste. She's consuming me, her lips moving with mine without hesitation.

"Whoa." Someone calls out, and we break apart, staring at each other before she turns to my new enemy because whoever interrupted that kiss deserves to get blacklisted.

Avery's chest rises and falls rapidly, and her cheeks are tinged red. I want to reach up and caress them, but I keep my hands to myself because a young woman is staring at us with surprise and humor.

"Well, that's one way to shut down the rumors."

"Hey, Andrea, how are you?" Avery's voice is shaky.

"Not better than you, that's for sure." She giggles and looks over at me with interest. "Anyway, I was hoping you still had a cupcake left. I'll take one, and then you can go back to your Grinch." Her eyebrows waggle.

Avery groans, hands her the cupcake, and then charges her.

"Toodles!" She waves her fingers and walks away.

"Andrea works at the school with Lizzy," Avery explains as if I care. The only thing I care about right now is getting her alone.

"Sorry about...the kiss. Matthew kept looking at us, and I think he overheard me tell Lizzy and Dani that we weren't really in a relationship, so I acted on the impulse to prove him wrong."

"You think he overheard?" I lift my brows.

"Okay, he did and questioned me, *but* I did a great job of covering it up by saying we aren't one of those couples who match our outfits." She cringes.

"That's hilarious because he and Jessy are matching." I laugh.

"I know." She slaps my arm. "I didn't know that when I made up the excuse, and she showed up right after. It was horrible." She giggles and covers her mouth, eyes widening.

"For what it's worth..." I shift to stand close to her, my hands landing on her hips. "I don't hate that you kissed me."

Avery's lips part. I want to take her bottom one between my teeth, but I will control myself in public. We already had an audience for our first kiss.

"Do you?" I tilt my head when she remains silent.

She shakes her head. "I should regret it."

"I'm glad you don't," I whisper, lifting a hand and brushing her cheek, finally allowing myself to touch her.

Avery sighs, closing her eyes.

"How much longer do you have here?" My eyes burn into hers.

I want to get her alone to talk openly and kiss her some more.

14

AVERY

I MAY HAVE LOST my mind, but as soon as I can, I clean up my stand and rush to the bakery with Gabriel to drop off the containers. That kiss left me buzzing for more.

"Oof," Gabriel calls out, stumbling back.

"Sorry." I look at him in the dark bakery where I just ran into him.

I reach out and switch the light on, finding a smile on his face. Without saying a word, he grabs my hips and pulls me toward him, his lips smashing against mine. My arms wrap around his shoulders, leaning into him as our lips meld.

Everything inside of me bursts. My skin tingles, and the hairs on my arms stand as chills race down my spine in the best way possible. Gabriel slows the kiss, adding a layer of sensuality to it as he lazily explores my mouth.

When the costume starts to itch my arms, I push back and search for the Velcro that opens his costume.

"Whoa." Gabriel chuckles. "You wanna fast forward?"

"The material is making me itch. I was just wanting to be able to kiss you without breaking out in a rash."

"Oh. Hold on." He undoes the Velcro and slowly pushes the costume down his arms and torso.

My eyes trail his defined chest and abs, taking in every inch.

"Like what you see?" Gabriel's voice rings with humor.

"Huh?" My eyes snap up to his face. "Uh, yeah." I nod because who am I to deny that the man is hot?

He throws on the shirt he was wearing earlier, much to my disappointment, and grips the back of my neck, kissing me fervently. If this is all we did all night long, I wouldn't have a single complaint. His warmth is addicting, and the way his stubble scratches against my skin is dizzying.

"Gabe," I moan.

"Yeah, Rudolph?" I feel him smile against my lips.

"You kiss really well."

He laughs, holding my face a few inches from his. "Thanks."

"No, no, thank you." I hold the back of his head and kiss him again.

Then, his lips move down my jaw and to my neck, making me break out in goosebumps. My entire body perks up as his lips kiss the sensitive spot beneath my ear. When he takes my earlobe between his teeth, I shiver and moan.

I can't even deny it. I want this man badly.

"Upstairs," I mumble.

"Are you sure? We can take it slow." Gabriel lifts his head to look at me.

"I'm positive." I'm breathless and full of desire.

Grabbing his hand, I drag him out of the bakery, turning off the lights and hastily locking the door before leading him up to my apartment.

Once the door closes behind us, I turn to look at him with a shy smile. Gabriel looks around my small home before his eyes land on mine.

"You really love Christmas, huh?"

My apartment is decked out in decorations, from a tree in my living area to lights strung along my TV stand with gnomes on it. A Santa sits on the coffee table with a small tree-shaped plate holding chocolate kisses.

"I do." I shrug and walk farther in, unsure of how to resume our make-out session.

"Come here." Thankfully, Gabe seems to know what to do.

I walk toward him with a smile. His hands grip my waist, his thumbs brushing along my ribs. His eyes shift from mine to my lips and back up.

"The moment I saw you, I noticed how beautiful you are, but you turned that sass on me and closed yourself up. I'll have to thank Matthew for showing up and leading you to call me your boyfriend because it's made it possible for me to get to know you. And do you know what I think?" His voice is deep.

I shake my head.

"That you're more beautiful than I originally thought because it's not just looks but your heart and mind, and I'm so glad you're no longer married so I can do this." He leans in and steals my breath with a searing kiss.

Words aren't necessary as our lips and hands explore as much as we can. Blindly, I lead him toward my bedroom. When my legs hit the bed, I sit and look up at him.

Gabriel's eyes burn with a fire so hot, I think it'll crisp a marshmallow just by getting near it. His hands roam down my arms and reach my hands, lacing our fingers together. I hold my breath, waiting for his next move.

After a few beats, he continues down to the hem of my sweater, tearing it up my body. He steps back and admires me, eyes blazing even more. He kneels in front of me, unzipping my boots and removing them one by one.

I can't help but notice how ridiculous he looks in his shirt and green tights, but it does nothing to hide the way he's feeling. His erection is plain as day.

"Stand up." His demand is stern, and I follow orders.

His fingers caress my skin from my shoulders to my ribs and stomach. My muscles contract at the ticklish sensation. When he reaches my skirt, he looks at me, asking for confirmation with his eyes. I nod, encouraging him.

"I want this," I say in case there's any doubt.

If all this turns out to be is a Christmas fling, then I'll enjoy it for what it is.

He's gentle as he slides my skirt down my legs. It's all happening in slow motion, as if adding to my torture. I've never been very patient, less so in a moment like this.

My fingers go to his shirt but pause.

"Sorry, but the tights really need to go." I shake with laughter.

"I think I'm a trendsetter." He stretches his leg out.

"No, please." I shake my head, tears building in my eyes as I continue to laugh.

"I know what it is. You just want to see me naked." He waggles his eyebrows. "As you wish." He tears the tights off and sighs. "I don't know how you women wear those."

"Beauty is pain."

"Actually, beauty is *you* naked," he growls, wrapping his arms around me and tossing us both on the bed.

I laugh beneath him, a sense of peace and happiness spreading through me.

"You're ridiculous."

"But sexy." He nips my collarbone.

"Yeah." I sigh.

Reaching for his shirt, I move it up his body, once again getting an eyeful of his muscles. His arms flex as he holds his weight off me, and I want to kiss every inch of him.

"I need you." He kisses me again, hands no longer shy as they move to more intimate areas.

When his fingers sneak into my underwear, I moan in pleasure. They brush against my clit, and my hips buck up. To say I'm sensitive is an understatement. Gabriel smirks and moves his lips to my neck, kissing me slowly as he inches his fingers into me.

He takes his time to pleasure me, building this burning need waiting to unravel.

"I want to hear you moan and beg." His voice is hoarse. "Tell me what you need." He sucks my earlobe.

"More of that. Fuck me with your fingers and stroke my clit. Give me everything you've got."

"Darling, this is just the beginning. Everything would rattle this bed."

"Then give me that," I challenge.

He growls, taking my lips in his again and kissing me with desperation. I reach out and tug his underwear down hastily. Wrapping my hand around his length, Gabriel groans into my mouth and pushes his hips into my touch.

I stroke him evenly, but when his fingers curl in my pussy, my movements falter.

"Fall for me. I need to be witness to it." His words fuel me on, and I try to catch my breath, but it's impossible.

He's making me feel out of control as I thrash on the bed, releasing his cock to lose myself in the orgasm. Colors swirl behind my eyelids as I fall into an ocean of pleasure. My skin pebbles and he leans his head toward my chest, taking a nipple in his mouth through my bra.

I'm not even fully naked, and he's making me fall apart. What kind of Christmas witchery is this?

"Gorgeous." He kisses my cheek once I've come undone and then rubs his nose along my skin.

I reach behind me to unsnap my bra. His eyes darken as I expose myself to him. He strips off my underwear, and I lie here for him to admire. Gabriel settles with his legs on either side of my thighs and softly runs his finger from my throat down the center of my body to my pelvis. Meanwhile, I can't ignore his hard cock so close to where I want him.

I sit up and scoot forward, almost knocking him off to the side. Without an apology, I open the drawer of my nightstand and take out a condom.

"I don't think this came with your costume." I hold up the foil packet.

Growling, he steals it from me and then aligns himself with my body. He brushes my hair away, and that's when I realize I've probably lost the neatly placed bobby pin holding my bangs back. A flash of panic strikes me, but before I can react, he pushes into me, causing me to moan out in pleasure.

Gabriel moves with languid strokes as I adjust to him. Then, I buck my hips, matching his movements, so we create our own rhythm. My nails dig into his back as we kiss wildly. The movements go from measured and controlled to chaotic desperation. My heart bangs in my chest, but the sensation isn't formed by nerves but by need.

He's come into my life to turn it upside down, and in him, I've found solace. What a strange turn of events.

I arch my back when he hits that spot that makes me tremble. Gabriel pushes into me harder, making us both feel a plethora of sensations. I hold on to him, moaning and losing myself. I spiral down again, pressure building until I can't hold back anymore, and I'm forced to call out his name.

Gabriel thrusts, prolonging my orgasm until he stills inside of me, kissing my shoulder and then my lips. It's a sweet gesture in turn to what we just did, and I fall for him a little bit more from how he can be so gentle after taking me so wildly.

"Wow," he breathes out, moving to lie beside me.

"Yeah." I sigh.

"We're gonna have to do that again soon."

I laugh and turn to look at him. He brushes my hair out of my face and smiles. I close my eyes for a moment, feeling like I'm on top of the world.

When I blink my eyes open again, he's looking at me with a softness that steals my breath. Maybe this could be more than a Christmas fling with my Grinch.

15

AVERY

THE LAST FEW DAYS have been magical. Spending time with Gabe has been amazing, and I'm enjoying getting to know him outside of the bakery. We spent the Sunday after the Christmas festival lazily lying in bed and getting much more acquainted. Let me tell you, he knows how to use his mouth and hands in ways that drive me wild.

We had lunch and walked around town like a real couple. I want to believe it could be true, but in three days, he's leaving for Denver for Christmas and to return to his real life whether I sell to him or not.

Meanwhile, I'll be here wondering if meeting him was all part of a Christmas dream. Maybe it's the ghost of Christmas future showing me what my life could be like in a positive light.

"Are you just going to stare off all day or actually do some work? You know, if I were your boss, I'd have to lecture you on productivity and focus."

I turn around with a smile and cross my arms.

"If you were my boss, we wouldn't have done what we did this morning." I stand tall and lift a brow.

"Ah, so you don't like boss and employee role play. Noted." He winks. "How about Grinch and Rudolph?"

I spit out laughing and shake my head. "Please do not ruin Christmas characters for me with a freaky kink."

Gabriel laughs and wraps me in his arms, kissing the top of my nose.

"It's just because I like you so much." His lips brush mine, and I relax into him. "I kind of don't want to leave on Friday."

I bite my lip because I feel the same, but it's selfish to voice it. He has a life outside of this snow globe we've created.

"I know." My voice is tight.

"We'll figure it out." He kisses my forehead and taps my butt. "Now, let's get to work."

"Are you still trying to buy the bakery from me? Because these last few days felt more like we were partners than competitors." I have to know the answer to this.

Gabriel has helped me so much, but not in the way he originally offered. Instead of telling me everything he'd do to make this business better, he's just flowed with me and given me honest suggestions that could increase my clientele.

"I want a location in Emerald Bay. It's been a dream for a few years."

My shoulders tense. Are we back to the beginning?

"But this is your baby, and I can't take it from you. Not now. Not even if I'm doing it fairly, even if you agreed to sell. I just couldn't." He runs a hand through his hair.

I reach for the hand tearing his hair, intertwining my fingers with his. My eyes bore into his as I smile softly.

"Thank you for being honest from the beginning. After what happened with Matthew, where I thought our relationship was still going strong, and then he blindsided me with his desire to divorce, I've been afraid of letting anyone in. Afraid I'd be blind to the truth in a relationship."

His smile comforts me. "You don't need to worry about that. We didn't get off on the right foot, but I've been open about why I came here and what I was looking for. Now, I can guarantee that the reason has changed. You're what I want."

I lean up on my toes and kiss him.

"Time for work." He cradles my face a moment before stepping back.

I wonder if I can just remain closed all day and spend time with him. Take a Christmas vacation.

The morning progresses with a bit more business than I've been experiencing, and I'm glad people are letting go of gossip and returning to buy here.

In between customers, Gabriel finds ways to brush against me, squeeze my hand, and caress my fingers. It's a slow, sensual build-up with innocent touches that spark the fire he's lit.

I head to the kitchen to grab a chocolate cake since someone took the whole one I usually sell by the slice. Walking behind the counter, my foot slips on something, and I crash into Gabriel, smashing the cake on his apron.

"No! Oh my fuckity fuck." I unstick the ruined cake from him, wanting to cry.

There is nothing worse than wasted cake.

"It's okay." He rushes to say, squeezing my shoulders, but his shoulders shake.

"It's not funny!" I slap his arm.

"I know, sorry. I can make another one." His voice cracks with laughter.

"Gabe." I look up at him to see his eyes filled with humor.

I set the cake down on the counter and shake my head. Things were going so well today.

"You're allowed to laugh at disasters, Rudolph." Gabriel grabs my hands and shakes my arms as if they were noodles.

"Release that stress. If people don't have chocolate cake today, that's okay. You sold out. How amazing is that?" His smile is so wide that it's contagious.

"It is pretty awesome that she wanted the whole cake. And I got a good aim on you, Grinch."

"That's my girl." He pulls me in for a hug, and I shove him away. "Don't dirty my apron."

"With this?" He runs a finger through the frosting-stained fabric and holds up a glob of frosting.

"Gabe," I warn with a palm out.

He licks his fingers and moans. "I have to admit that your frosting is better than mine."

"That sounds dirty," I laugh.

"Did you say you want to get dirty?" He swipes another chunk of frosting and comes toward me.

"Don't," I beg, backing away.

When he leaps, I make a run for it, but my foot slips again, causing me to land on the floor. Gabriel topples on top of me, smearing frosting on my face and laughing.

"You're in trouble, mister!"

"I thought I was the Grinch," he retorts.

I push my hand between us, grabbing frosting and smearing it on his cheek. Laughing, I try to slide away from him, but his strong arms hook around me and keep me in place.

"No escaping me." His voice is husky.

"That was payback." I fight against him, but my laughter makes my movements jerky and weak.

"I've got your payback."

"Hello?" We both look up to see a neighbor on the other side of the counter, looking down at us with eyebrows raised in shock.

"Uh, hi." I scramble to my feet, slipping again. My face heats as I look down at the tile. "The floor here is dirty. We fell." What in the hell is on the floor? It must be oil or something. Maybe butter.

The woman just stares at me—unblinking—while my heart races as if I ran a million miles.

"I'll clean the floor," Gabriel says as he walks into the kitchen with the destroyed cake.

"You have frosting here." The woman points to her cheek.

"Right." I scramble to grab my apron and wipe my face.

This is my most unprofessional experience, and instead of wanting to hide, laughter bubbles at the base of my throat.

Gabriel comes out of the kitchen with a clean apron and a mop. When I read the apron, I burst out laughing, no longer able to hold back. It says, *Queen of the Kitchen*.

"It was the only clean apron I could find." Gabriel doesn't seem one bit bothered.

"You wear it well." The customer laughs quietly and winks at me.

One thing I've learned since meeting Gabriel is to not take myself too seriously. The world won't explode if things don't go according to plan. I used to live like that, too, and then the divorce happened, and all these insecurities surfaced.

It's time I return to my true self. The one who lived freely and happily.

16
GABRIEL

"Is it weird living here where it doesn't snow?" I ask Avery as we walk along the cold sand on the beach.

The waves crash against the shore, creating a playlist for the late afternoon. The sky reflects hues of orange and red.

"It was in the beginning. I missed having a white Christmas and the freezing temperatures, but it was nice to not have to shovel snow or deal with the ugly, dirty snow when it's been on the ground for days." Her face is illuminated under the setting sun.

Avery takes my breath away. Everything from her drive to her kind heart pulls me in. I'm not ready to leave her, but with no business in the area, how can I make this work? I've been tossing options around for the last couple of days so we can continue to build our relationship.

Some people might say I'm insane for making life changes for a woman I just met, but she feels like home. The other night we crossed carolers on the street, and Avery joined them for a song. She was singing so happily and freely. It showed me another side of the woman I'm falling for.

"That makes sense."

"I got used to it, and Emerald Bay is paradise." She points toward the beach.

"It is." I nod, looking out at the ocean. "I have so many great memories here."

"I believe it."

We pause near the shore but far enough to not get our feet wet. This may be Florida, but it's still cold, and the water is freezing. Avery turns toward me and squeezes my hand.

"I have a Friendsmas dinner tomorrow. Would you want to come with me? Luke will be there as well, so it's not just a girls' night." She chews on her bottom lip, so I lift my thumb and remove it.

"I'd love to." I bow my head to kiss her. "Let's go have dinner."

She nods and pulls me away from the soothing ocean, but I have my own paradise in her. Everything I love about Emerald Bay is muted in comparison to her. She's the light in this town now. The beaming light that I'm drawn to. My Northern star guiding the way.

"Let's go to Bayside. Are you too cold to sit on the deck?" She challenges me with a smile.

"I'm from Colorado. You're the Florida transplant."

"I can handle the cold."

"Right, Rudolph," I tease her. "And they have heating towers, so you'll be comfortable."

"Very true." She nods.

"Romantic dinner for two by the ocean coming right up." I twirl her around, causing her to laugh. It's the best sound in the world.

"Are you excited to see your brother?" Avery asks as we share a molten chocolate cake after dinner. It's not as good as the destroyed chocolate cake we shared yesterday after closing the bakery, but I'm sharing it with her, and that's all that matters.

People at the restaurant haven't hidden their curiosity despite seeing us together at the bakery and around town. I'm definitely not used to small-town gossip and expected it to last a few days before people moved on.

"I am. It's been a while since I've seen him, so it'll be nice but..." I hesitate.

"What?" She tilts her head.

I place my spoon on the edge of the plate and reach for her free hand. Looking into her round eyes, I smile.

"I'm going to miss you. This wasn't part of my plans, but now that I've met you, the thought of leaving crushes me." I lay my heart out there. So much for being a Grinch.

Her gaze softens, and she leans forward, resting her elbow on the table and turning my hand over, tracing the lines on my palm.

"I'm going to miss you, too." Her head bows, gaze landing on the table for a beat. When she looks up at me again, sadness swims in her eyes. "I was so not looking to meet anyone. When my friends teased me that you could be a potential partner, I laughed and tossed that idea away. One, you were here to buy me out. Two, I was over the idea of love. One failed marriage is enough to last me forever, and the thought of going through that again was too much to even consider."

She takes a deep breath, looking at my hand. I want to say so many things, but nothing I say would be enough to comfort her. I've never been through a divorce, so I don't know how it feels.

"We never know what the future holds. Nothing in life is guaranteed, not even life itself, but I can promise you that what

I'm feeling is real. Whether the town is watching or we're alone, this is no longer about convincing you to sell. I don't want Sprinkles of Joy. It's yours. You deserve it." I lift her hand and kiss the top of it. She shivers, her lips parting.

Her eyes lift beneath her eyelashes, and heat flashes across them. If I only have a couple of days with her, I want to spend each moment loving her. When I'm gone, I don't want her to doubt what I feel or think this is just a Christmas romance. We have the potential to be so much more...

I just need to get some things in order first.

17

AVERY

"Nooo. You cheated!" Dani accuses Luke of knocking down our plastic cup Christmas tree tower. We were racing to see who could stack cups to create a tall triangle tree the fastest.

"No way. That was all you, but we win." He smirks.

I chuckle between them at their competitiveness and catch Gabriel's eyes.

"I want a rematch." Dani shakes her head.

We played guys versus girls—Gabriel, Luke, and Erik—another friend—against Lizzy, Dani, Andrea, and me.

"And I need another glass of sangria." Lizzy stands, walking to the kitchen in Dani's house.

"Me too." I follow behind her.

Dani's sangria is the best. It's her dad's recipe, and she makes it at every gathering we have.

"Things look like they're going great with Gabriel." Lizzy leans against the counter after we get a refill and sips her drink.

"They are. He's great, despite my original belief."

"I'm happy to hear that."

"How are you? With the whole Sean thing." I purse my lips. She says she's okay, but I wonder if it's true.

"I'm honestly okay. It sucks, but I've realized how different we are now that we're not together. I'm going to enjoy my single life, which means hanging out with my friends, reading books, eating whenever the hell I want, and living in pajamas when I'm not at work. Sean believes pajamas are just for sleeping, not to lounge in." She rolls her eyes.

"You mean he expected you to be dressed impeccably after working all day?" Sarcasm drips from my words.

"I know. Who the hell keeps their shoes on at home?" She chuckles and straightens. "Anyway, I'm good and will be completely over it soon. My mom's relieved. She never really liked him." She shrugs.

"Are you ladies coming back?" Dani calls out from the living room.

"Be right there." We giggle and stay in the kitchen, talking.

By the time we return to the living room, the guys are leaning back in their seats, talking while Dani and Andrea neatly stack the cups. Gabriel reaches his arm out, so I go to him. When he tugs me onto his lap, I tense in surprise.

"Relax." He chuckles in my ear.

I do as he says and lean into him. Different conversations happen around us, and I try to follow each one, but I'm in my head. Gabriel leaves the day after tomorrow, and we don't live in a world where snowstorms happen in Florida. I don't think getting snowed in is an option. Even if it were, it'd just prolong the inevitable for a few days.

"How's business going?" Luke asks Gabriel.

"Great. I've got big plans I'm excited about."

I tense on his lap, wondering what he means. He told me he was no longer interested in buying Sprinkles of Joy or opening a Sweet Delights location in town.

His hand squeezes my hip, but I don't look at him. Instead, I focus on the conversation the girls are having. Lizzy is telling them that she's getting a new student in January—one who's coming from Texas.

I try to listen as doubts roll in my stomach while Gabriel talks to Luke and Erik. What does he mean by "big plans?" Potential ideas swirl in my head. I don't want to think he lied to me.

Taking a deep breath, I excuse myself to go to the bathroom. I walk in and stare at my reflection, deciding to release my bangs and comb them down on my forehead. They're still a disaster. I clip them back and then stare into my eyes.

"Gabriel isn't Matthew. He's been honest from the start. Don't sabotage the time you have left."

He could've meant something else. Maybe he has other business plans that have nothing to do with Emerald Bay.

A knock echoes on the door, and I take a deep breath before opening it. Gabriel stands before me with furrowed brows.

"Are you okay?"

"I'm great." I smile. "Wonderful." I clap my hands way too hard, causing my palms to tingle.

"You sure?" He tilts his head.

"Positive." I need to let go of the past and let this play out the way it does. I pray it doesn't end up in heartbreak.

"Okay." He reaches for my hand and takes me back out to the living room.

We leave a little while later. I have to be up early to open the bakery, and Gabriel has some errands to run in the morning. It's another reminder that he'll be gone soon.

He walks me up to my apartment, and we stare at each other outside the door. He reaches for my hand and smiles.

"Are you sure you're okay?"

"Yeah."

"If you say so, Rudolph." He taps my nose. "I'll see you tomorrow then."

"Do you want to stay?" I unlock the door and push aside doubts and fears, my vulnerability showing.

"I thought you'd never ask." He wraps his arm around my waist and kisses me, his other hand moving behind me to open the door.

Every thought evaporates as his tongue pushes past my lips, claiming me in a searing kiss that makes my toes curl. My body reacts to him with chills running down my spine and heat bubbling in my belly.

We stumble into my apartment, tearing each other's clothes off. When his shirt comes off, I roam my hands down his chest and abs, loving the way his muscles twitch under my touch.

His hands go to my ribs, and I giggle at the ticklish sensation. But my laughter catches when he unsnaps my bra and palms my breasts, twisting my nipples. My head falls back on a moan, and he takes the opportunity to kiss my neck. It's all too much.

"Bedroom," he grunts against my skin.

"Yeah," I say breathlessly.

We make our way into my room, falling onto the mattress in a heap of hands and mouths, exploring each other. It doesn't take long for him to bring me to the brink with his mouth. I've decided that Gabriel's mouth on my sensitive body is the most divine thing in the world. More than chocolate cake.

"If I had frosting, I'd smear it on you and clean you up with my tongue."

I shiver at his suggestion, wishing I had some in the fridge so he could keep his promise.

"You liked that idea, huh?" He slides up my body, kissing me hard and fast.

"We can make that happen one day," I retort. "Only if we take turns." I wrap my arms around his back, bringing his weight down on me and kissing him deeply.

He groans and reaches into my nightstand. We stare at each other for a moment, taking a second from the desperation to feel the moment. He places his hand over my heart and smiles.

"I want this."

I nod, swallowing thickly. I refuse for my earlier concerns to ruin this moment, so I lift my head and kiss him. He enters me slowly, taking his time so that we both feel every second of pleasure. My walls clench around him as he fills me completely.

We move slowly, taking our time as if we're afraid the moment will slip from our grasp. Gabriel grabs my waist and turns over, positioning me on top of him.

"Let me see you ride me." His voice is gruff.

Placing my hands on his chest, I lift my body and rock over him. He sits up, taking my nipple between his teeth, causing pleasure and pain in a combustive combination. I toss my head back on a moan, my hair hitting the base of my spine.

I lose myself in him, living in the present. I forget about the bakery, my struggles, and the pain of the past. Right now, Gabriel is all I see, hear, smell, feel, and taste. He's my five senses. He's consumed me in such a way that there's no turning back.

It terrifies me and excites me at the same time.

I've willingly given my heart to the Grinch, and I can't find it in me to regret it.

18
GABRIEL

I kiss Avery for the millionth time before climbing into the cab that's patiently waiting for me outside of the bakery. I hate leaving her, but we both knew it would come to this.

"I'll call you when I land."

She nods sadly.

"Smile, Rudolph." I lift the corner of her lips with my thumb. It grants me the smile I'm seeking, but it doesn't last long. I promised her this wasn't goodbye, but it feels like it.

"Have a safe trip." She squeezes my hand.

"I will." I need to get back to Denver so that I can figure out if it's possible to run my bakeries while living here. I have managers who handle the day-to-day in each location, but I'm a control freak and like to check in personally every week.

Sometimes, though, priorities change. Sweet Delights has been running successfully for some years now. This could be the moment to make a change. It's worth it for the woman in front of me.

"Bye, Grinch." She kisses my cheek.

"See ya, Rudolph." I get into the cab before I regret leaving.

The ride to the airport is long. My knee bounces as I wish it were closer so I could already be back in Denver and putting the pieces into action. My phone rings, and I answer.

"Hey, bro," Ben says as soon as the call connects.

"Hey, what's going on?"

"Nothing. Wondering at what time you get in."

"I land at six. You'll pick me up?"

"You know it. We can grab a drink before heading home." He's staying at my place while he's in town—much to my mom's disappointment because she wants to hog his time anytime he's there.

"Yeah, that's a great idea, actually. I could use a drink now." I run a hand down my face.

"What's going on?"

"Nothing. We'll talk when I get there." I really don't want to talk about a woman over the phone in the back of a taxi. For all I know, the cab driver knows Avery and will tell the town all about my conversation.

"Sounds good. I'll see you later, then."

We hang up, and I lean back in the seat. This is going to be the longest day. I wish I were back at Sprinkles of Joy with Avery, baking and sneaking kisses in between customers.

"You say you're fine, but you keep staring at your phone in frustration," Ben says.

"I am fine." I grab my scotch and take a drink, the warm liquid doing nothing to clear my mind.

I sent Avery a message that I had arrived and still haven't heard from her. It was almost an hour ago. I know the bakery is closed, so I'm not sure what's going on, but I hate it because I'm afraid she's in her head.

"I call bull." My brother scoffs.

I release a heavy exhale and level him with my gaze. Usually, I'm forthcoming with information, but I'm not sure why I want to keep Avery to myself. If I want a chance to be with her, then I need to bring her into my life, even if just by talking about her.

"I met someone," I confess.

"I knew it." He slaps the bar top.

Unlike people in Emerald Bay who would turn to look at us to see what's going on, no one in this bar cares. It's a huge difference between living in a big city and a small town.

I tell him about Avery. How we met, who she is, and what I feel for her. Ben's eyebrows shoot up, and he shakes his head.

"You wanted to buy her out? Classic enemies-to-lovers stuff right there."

"Excuse me?" I stare at him.

"Enemies-to-lovers. It's a trope in romance. Whatever." He waves me off, looking away.

"No, you don't. How do you know that? What the hell is a trope?"

"It's a plot in romance movies and books. I've been reading romance lately. You should give it a try. It's like a manual of what women want." He smirks.

"I don't need a manual."

"Clearly, you do if you're sitting here telling me about your sorrows and waiting for a woman to respond to your message." He chuckles, shaking his head as if I were an idiot.

"Whatever," I mumble, drinking my scotch.

"Honestly, romance novels are great."

"How did you even get into it?" Curiosity gets the best of me.

"A co-worker dared me to read one, and I got hooked on the genre." He leans back on his stool, drinking his gin and tonic.

"A co-worker?" I lift my brows.

"We're just friends."

"Uh, huh." I finish off what's left of my drink and push the glass away.

"So what are you going to do about Avery?"

"I don't want to give up on what we have. I've thought about moving to Emerald Bay. My locations are spread out in different cities, so even living here means I have to travel. What difference does it make if I live here or in Florida?" He's the first person I have told of my plans, and nerves get the best of me waiting for his reaction.

"Whoa. Does she know you want to do that?"

"No. I wanted it to be a surprise."

"Ah, the grand gesture." He nods in approval.

"The what?" My face scrunches up.

"The grand gesture. The big event to show the woman you love her. I know what I'm going to give you for Christmas—a romance novel. Do yourself a favor and read it." He huffs out as if I'm a disappointment to him.

"Anyway, I was hoping to take care of a few things while I'm here for Christmas and return before the new year. I have Grandma and Grandpa's house, so it's not an impossible feat." It feels good to voice this and hear the plan out loud. I've been unsure if it's right or wrong, but my heart's in it, so that has to mean something.

By the time we finish our drinks, I feel lighter.

"Ready to go?" I clap his back.

"Yeah. Let's get out of here. Mom's going to be pissed if we're late for dinner. I promised her I'd take you straight to their house, so say the flight got delayed or security thought you were a criminal and kept you hostage for a couple hours."

"Nice try." I laugh.

Despite Christmas Eve happening in two days, my mom practically forced us to have dinner with them tonight before the craziness of the holidays begins with our entire family.

"I'll tell her that brotherly bonding time comes before anything else. Are you going to tell them about your plans?" He lifts a brow.

"And ruin their Christmas? I'm their favorite because I stayed in Denver. No way. I'm going to wait until after."

"You're an ass." He punches my shoulder and then hooks his arm around my neck. "Let's go, big brother."

Feeling grateful I have him on my side, I walk out of the bar with a clearer idea of what I want. If only Avery would respond to me. Once I'm done with dinner, I'm calling her until she picks up the phone.

19
AVERY

Business is back to usual at Sprinkles of Joy, and maybe Gabriel was my Christmas miracle for that purpose. But I miss him. We've spoken in the last two days, and he talks as if we've got a future, but I don't see how.

The entire town is buzzing with Christmas joy today as they prepare for Christmas Eve dinner. I'll be spending a quiet evening at home with some pasta and a mini mint chocolate cake I made this morning.

It's a sad excuse for a Christmas Eve, but my family is far away, and it's my first Christmas not married to Matthew. I told my parents not to worry about traveling down here. Although Lizzy and Dani both invited me to dinner at their houses, I wasn't up for it.

I want to be alone, watch *The Holiday,* and pretend my long-distance relationship can turn out like the movie. I look at the angel on my tree and tell it my wish. It worked when I asked for business to improve.

As I finish packaging the last of my orders, I wait for those customers to come pick them up before closing. I won't open tomorrow, and it'll be nice to sleep in and wallow. I never thought someone would steal my heart like this after what happened with Matthew, and it's like the universe accepted my challenge and proved me wrong.

The entire town will be with loved ones, and some people will walk around in the afternoon, so it's the perfect excuse to have a lazy day.

My phone buzzes, and I grab it, seeing a message from Gabriel.

> Grinch: Merry Christmas Eve, Rudolph. Thinking of you. How are you?

> Me: Merry Christmas Eve to you, too, Grinch. I'm good. Finishing up at the bakery soon and then spending a quiet evening with a holiday movie and cake.

> Me: Are you having fun with your family?

> Grinch: Yeah but I wish you were here. Or I was there. My brother's driving my mom crazy and it's fun to watch. She pretends she hates it but secretly loves it.

> Me: I'm sure she does.

Grinch: I need to help my dad set up some tables but I wanted to check in with you. I'll call you later. We can video chat.

Me: Enjoy time with your family. Don't worry about me.

Grinch: Not gonna happen, Rudolph. You're on my mind 24/7.

Me: <kiss emoji>

Talking to him makes me happy and gives me hope that his departure wasn't the end. It seems impossible at the moment, but maybe things can turn out differently.

I sigh when the last order is picked up and lean against the locked door. I'm glad I started cleaning before closing time, so I could leave sooner. All I have left to do is set the dishwasher in the kitchen and mop the front of the store. When I finish, I take my dessert upstairs and then head out to take a walk through town before going home again.

I inhale the fresh air, feeling the saltiness hit my nose. Releasing a breath, I walk down the center of town toward the boardwalk. I cross a few people taking a stroll in the afternoon before they have dinner and greet them as we pass each other.

Reaching the boardwalk, I see a couple out on the sand facing the water. The man has his arms wrapped around the woman's body. The closer I get, the clearer they become, and I realize it's Matthew. My heart constricts for a moment and then releases the last bit of pain from the past. It washes away like the waves. I really hope he's happy. It's all I've ever wished for him. Our divorce may have blindsided me, but I wish him no harm. Never have, even when I was heartbroken.

Walking away, I head to the left and take in the colorful storefronts that make this part of town so beautiful. I lose track of time as I wander silently, clearing my head and focusing on my future. When the sun starts to descend, I head back home for a quiet night in pajamas.

Do you know what's worse than crooked bangs? Calling the guy you love after missing his video call the night before only for him not to answer. Numerous times. I've talked myself out of calling or messaging him again, more than I would like to admit, because *crazy girlfriend* is not my cup of tea.

So, I'm at the bakery, getting my emotions out by kneading dough and rolling it out forcefully.

It's Christmas Day. He's with his family. Let him enjoy it.

My phone rings across the kitchen, and I wipe my hands on my apron and run to grab it. I frown when I see my mom's name. I love her, but I really wish it were Gabriel. Besides, we've already spoken. Three times in the last two days. I get that she's worried about me, though. She's likely wishing she were here so I wouldn't spend the holiday alone.

"Hi, Mom."

"Hi, sweetie. What are you up to?"

"Baking." I walk back to the island and resume my rolling with the phone tucked between my ear and neck.

"You don't open today."

"No, I'm baking for myself. I was in the mood for sugar cookies." I grab my Christmas cookie cutters and begin cutting candy canes, trees, snowmen, and stars out of the dough, placing them on the cookie sheet.

"Are you sure you're okay? You haven't sounded like yourself lately." Worry rings through the phone.

"I am, promise." I smile in hopes that it brightens my voice.

"Your father and I are thinking of heading down to see you after the holidays."

"Why?" I pause what I'm doing.

"What do you mean, why? Because you're our daughter, and we love you and want to see you." She goes full-blown mama bear.

"Got it," I say. "I didn't mean it in a bad way." I giggle and shake my head.

"I know. We miss you, though. You think you can make time for us?" Her voice turns teasing.

"As if I have a choice," I joke.

"Avery Bailey," she chastises.

"Just kidding, Mom. I'd love for you guys to come visit me. You know the bakery doesn't give me much time to take a vacation."

"That's why we thought we'd come down to you."

Distant pounding sounds through the bakery, distracting me. What in the world is going on? There's no road work going on, especially on a holiday like today.

"Mom, can I call you back?" I start to walk to the front of the store, but I don't see anything out the windows. Opening the door, I listen to see if I hear anything.

"Sure, sweetie. Love you."

"Love you, too." I hang up and hear the banging again in the kitchen.

Checking the back door, it becomes louder. I step outside and look up at my apartment, stilling.

"Gabe?"

He turns around at the top of the stairs and smiles at me. Then he jogs down the steps and wraps his arms around me, spinning around. His lips land on mine, making everything click into place. There's nothing chaste or careful about it. He's demanding and persistent, kissing me as if it's been years.

"What are you doing here?" I lean my head back.

"I missed you."

I lift my brows and wait for him to say more than that. He laughs and squeezes me tightly again.

"Let's go upstairs and talk. Or are you baking?" He takes me in, wiping my cheek. Flour marks his thumb.

"I was baking, yes."

"Okay, let's go to the bakery then." He walks in as if he owns the place and closes the door behind us.

"I wasn't completely honest with you when I left."

The hairs on my neck stand as I hear his words.

"Not in a bad way," he quickly adds as if reading my reaction. "I had plans of returning to you by New Year's, but I wanted to make sure everything in Denver was taken care of before I got our hopes up and it couldn't happen. I want us to have a real shot, and I'm not very good at long-distance relationships. I'm greedy and need to see you daily." He smiles as I process his words.

"What are you saying?"

"I'm saying that I want to stay in Emerald Bay and be with you. Do you think you can handle the Grinch every day?" His eyes are hopeful.

"Every day?" I scrunch up my nose, holding back my smile. "I don't know."

His fingers go to my ribs, tickling me. "You liar."

I laugh, grabbing his hands and pulling them away.

"I am a liar. I don't think I can live without the Grinch for the rest of my life."

His gaze softens, and he leans forward, his lips millimeters from mine.

"I love you."

My eyes widen, but before I can respond, he lifts me and sits me on the counter, taking my lips with his. I wrap my arms around him, kissing him back. I have time to tell him how I feel afterward. Right now, I want to soak up this moment.

Breathing heavily, he leans back and grins. "I have a house here, and realistically, I have bakeries all throughout the country, so it's not like I would need to be in Denver all the time. Besides, I think you secretly love having me work with you."

"You know what I love?" I tilt my head and let my arms drape loosely over his shoulders. My legs tighten around his waist, and he arches an eyebrow. "Not that. Well, that too, but I love *you*, Grinch."

The smile that covers his face is blinding. His hands hold my cheeks, and he kisses me hard before staring into my eyes.

"Seeing my family last night, all happy and with loved ones, made me miss you more. I want to start my life with you, Avery. It might be crazy to other people, but I don't care what they think. I'm certain about what I feel for you."

"I am, too." I stroke his cheek, and he closes his eyes, breathing softly. He turns his face and kisses my palm before grabbing my hand.

"This is the best Christmas present," he tells me.

The last thing I expected when he strolled into this bakery was for me to fall in love with him. I was so against the idea of opening up to him at all, but he found a way to worm his way into my life and heart.

"How about we finish these cookies and take them upstairs with some frosting? I have a promise to keep." He squeezes my hips, eyes blazing.

"You've got yourself a deal, Grinch." I reach my hand out.

"I seal these types of deals with a kiss." He pushes into me, his mouth pressing to mine with the promise of many more deals to come.

EPILOGUE

AVERY

"Hello!" Gabriel saunters into Sprinkles of Joy with his arms extended, wearing his Grinch costume.

I stop wiping the counter and laugh.

"What do you think?" He looks down at himself.

"It's still as ridiculous as the first time I saw it." I shake my head, unable to get over the tights.

The kids in town loved the Santa and Grinch combination so much last year that Mrs. Barber decided to make it a new Emerald Bay tradition. And no one does Grinch better than my man.

This past year has been amazing with him. I never thought I'd fall in love again, and then this man waltzed into my life and won me over.

"I have something for you, too." He walks around the counter and holds out a reindeer antler headband. "It lights up and everything." He switches a button, and the antlers start to blink.

He places the antlers on my head and steps back. "Gorgeous. Keep it for the festival. It totally beats the Christmas hat." He leans in to kiss my cheek.

"Thanks." I laugh.

"No need to thank me." His hand sneaks under his coat. "I have something else for you."

"I don't think we have time for that," I tease.

"Not that." He shakes his head in exasperation. "I know you can't get enough of me, but this is something else." He winks.

"Cocky," I mutter.

"Always."

He pulls something from under the coat and drops to his knee. My eyes widen as I cover my mouth.

"Avery Rudolph Bailey." I snort at the name, but he continues talking. "I love you with my whole heart. I want to spend the rest of my life with you, baking together, laughing, singing, and building a family. Here, in the place that started our love story, the place where I fell in love with you, I have a simple question. Will you marry me?"

"Yes!" I scream. "A million times, yes."

He stands and wraps his arms around me, kissing me lazily. Then, he slides the most beautiful ring onto my finger. It's rose gold with a ruby in the center and a vintage design of accent diamonds all around the oval shape in two layers, making it almost look like a snowflake while more small diamonds go down the band on both sides.

"Wow." I take in the ring.

"I wanted something different and unique to you. Since you're my Rudolph and all." He winks.

"It's stunning." I glance up at him with a smile.

"I was nervous. I know you've been married once, and I thought maybe you'd reject my proposal and want to keep things the way they've been."

I shake my head, kissing him again. "I want this with you. You're my family, Gabe."

"Thank goodness." He sighs and then smiles. "Wanna get married tomorrow? The bakery is closed."

Laughing, I shove him playfully. "Nope. I want a wedding with our family and close friends. I want all that with you." I kiss him again.

"Our families are here for Christmas, sooo..." He lifts his brows.

"I may need a bit longer to plan, but it'll happen soon," I promise. "I actually have a proposal for you."

"Really? We have some time before the festival." He waggles his eyebrows.

"No, still can't take you seriously with this costume." I laugh and reach for my purse on the counter, pulling out a folder. I hand it to him and impatiently wait for him to read it.

"What is this?"

"Open it!" I urge him.

His eyes scan the document before looking up at me with wide eyes. "Are you sure?"

"Positive. You've been my partner this past year, making sure things run smoothly, working alongside me, and worrying along with me. I want this place to be both of ours." A year ago he walked in here wanting to buy my bakery. Today, I offer him a different kind of partnership, one where we both own the bakery.

"Sprinkles of Delight?" He grins widely.

"I think we'll keep the original name."

"It was worth a shot." He sighs playfully. "We're getting married."

"We are!" I jump on him and kiss him wildly as the reality of it all settles over me. "This is the best Christmas present ever. Totally beats last year's."

He laughs, kissing me deeply. I'm ready to spend many more Christmases with him, but most importantly, to continue building this life together.

Thank you for reading Avery and Gabriel's story! I hope you loved it. I'd appreciate if you left a short review on Amazon and Goodreads.

I can't wait for you to meet more of the Emerald Bay characters soon! Lizzy's story is now available! A swoony and steamy romantic comedy wrapped up in the quaint beach town of Emerald Bay.

What should you do when you accidentally call 911 and a deputy shows up at your apartment? Definitely NOT accuse him of being a stripper.

Read Guarded Deputy and find Fabiola's other books in the QR Code below!

THANK YOU!

Firstly, thank you for reading Kneading the Grinch! I've been so excited to write a holiday story, and this one came to me so quickly, that I knew I had to share it with you.

I've got an amazing bunch to thank, who have helped me make this release happen. Thank you to Victoria from Cruel Ink Editing and Bex from The Polished Author for editing and proofing this story!

Savannah, you're always there to listen to me freak out and celebrate my milestones. Thank you for your support and encouragement!

Daniele, thank you for reading an early copy and offering feedback. I'm so glad you're as excited as I am about these characters!

To my review team and master list, who always come through for me. THANK YOU for being the best supporters a girl could as for!

For my author friends who continue to cheer me on, we're in this together. I appreciate you so much.

For my readers, bloggers, and bookstagrammers, thank you for all the love you show me. I'm a lucky girl.

ABOUT FABIOLA FRANCISCO

Fabiola Francisco loves the escape books offer. She writes contemporary romance, mostly small town romances with swoony book boyfriends and strong and sassy heroines.

Writing has always been a part of her life, penning her own life struggles as a form of therapy through poetry. Now, she writes novels that will capture your heart and make feel a range of emotions.

She is continuously creating stories as she daydreams. She also enjoys country music, exploring the outdoors, and reading.

Printed in Great Britain
by Amazon